ENGAGED TO MURDER

ENGAGED TO MURDER

BY M. V. HEBERDEN

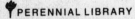

PERENNIAL LIBRARY
Harper & Row, Publishers
New York, Cambridge, Hagerstown, Philadelphia, San Francisco
London, Mexico City, São Paulo, Sydney

ENGAGED TO MURDER

CHAPTER 1

A marriage has been arranged and will take place shortly between Anne Mantle, daughter of the late Hugh and Elaine Mantle, and Henri Deschamps, Secretary of the French Embassy. Miss Mantle, who completed college in the United States three years ago, lives with her uncle, Howard Mantle, well known in Anglo-Argentine circles.

The announcement was in the Buenos Aires *Herald*, one of the two English-language newspapers. During the course of a damp, cold morning in winter a lot of people skimmed over the item while a few read it with close attention and varied reactions.

Stephen Sales, late U.S.N. and now manager of his father's factory in Argentina, stared at it in grim misery. Anne had told him herself, but somehow he had hoped that something would happen. Now that the formal announcement was in the paper, a final seal of despair was set on his hopelessness. He wondered, in the way that rejected suitors do, what she saw in the fellow. Henri Deschamps was amusing sometimes, admittedly, and gay with a certain febrile gaiety. Stephen Sales bit into his breakfast roll with savage energy. A lot of other women had been hanging round after the Frenchman too, he reflected, so he must have something.

Not that Stephen himself disliked him. Rather, he had not disliked him on the occasions on which he'd met him prior to the discovery that he was the chosen candidate. Now his feelings were mixed. He hoped Anne would be happy, he envied Henri his luck and he could cheerfully have choked him. Instead he finished his coffee and went to the office of his father's company, the Salsa Sales de Argentina, S.A., in Calle Cangallo.

Douglas Canning picked up the paper as he sat down to his solitary breakfast, easing himself rather carefully into the chair. He got through the news pages with his bacon and eggs, for though he was the fourth generation to be born in the Argentine, he still made an English breakfast. He was at his coffee when he skimmed over the society page. His blue eyes narrowed a little and instinctively turned to the stairs and the bedroom where his wife was still sleeping. Gloria did not get up to have breakfast with him.

He wondered if Gloria knew. His eyes reflected a certain weariness. He shouldn't have married her. It wasn't right to tie a woman to a man who took an hour to struggle into a brace every morning, who—— With a deliberate effort he stopped the train of thought; he'd been over it all so often. He also finished his coffee and left for his office.

It wasn't until some hours later that a maid penetrated into Gloria's room with the breakfast tray and the newspaper. She pushed back her shining copper hair and looked unwillingly at the tray, the clock, and the daylight. She remembered she was supposed to be driving her mother into town for lunch and wondered why she'd eaten those raw onions last night. They had been very good at the time, but right now she'd rather not remember them.

Gloria quite ignored the news pages of the *Herald*. She made straight for the center, the hatched, matched, dispatched page. Therefore, in less than a minute, she arrived at the notice. She read it twice before she really believed it. Her face hardened, and in spite of the clear skin and shining hair she looked almost plain. That was why he hadn't called up this week. So he thought she could be pushed on one side, did he, when he wanted to marry? She overlooked the fact that, as she herself was married, from her point of view Henri had always been something on the side. But then Gloria usually overlooked anything which wasn't convenient to look at. She did it with complete honesty, for she didn't even know she did it.

It never really occurred to her now that, as she had been amusing herself with Henri "on the side," there was no particular reason why he should not marry. She didn't think of it. She simply realized that she was about to be deprived of something she still wanted. She started to cry. It was not grief. It was anger.

Robert Fareham read *La Prensa* at breakfast, while his wife read the *Herald*. She suddenly said, "Well, what do you know about that?" and he looked up, knowing it was a signal that his attention was required. She read the piece to him.

"Deschamps is doing pretty nicely for himself," remarked Bob practically. "She'll come in for Mantle's money."

Louise Fareham was looking distressed. "But, Bob, I thought Anne and Steve Sales——" she stopped. "Let's have Steve for dinner and get that Martin girl. You know, the one who's just back from the States. With the cute nose."

Robert Fareham laughed. "Matchmaking already? Give Sales time to get over it. Or d'you think your candidate might get him on the rebound?"

"You never know. I *am* sorry for Steve."

"Wonder what Mantle thinks of Anne's choice?" He looked at his watch. "Time I went. 'By, darling. Don't try to marry Sales off before lunch."

Louise blew him a kiss. He always laughed at her matchmaking, though she wasn't very serious about it. Bob knew that. He'd known it for twenty-five years, bless his heart.

Dr. Alfredo Arrietti had quite a large practice among the Anglo-Argentine colony, and one of his patients showed him the paper, saying, "I don't think Mantle will like it."

Arrietti's face was impassive as he took the patient's blood pressure. He said, "No?"

"Deschamps is a lot older than Anne, to start with, and I don't think he's got a penny to his name, apart from what he earns in the Embassy."

The doctor didn't answer. He must call his old friend, Howard Mantle. He'd been rather worried about him recently.

Michel Fresne always read the social notes. He found it useful to know the gossip. He frowned at the notice for a while, a puzzled expression in his dark eyes. Deschamps . . . he hadn't met him. But Michel Fresne did not cultivate the society of the French Embassy crowd. Well, that ruled Anne Mantle out, anyway. Not that he minded much. In fact, he had realized some time ago that the pursuit of Anne would be waste of time. She was twenty-five and she regarded his forty-two years as something approaching senility.

So, in spite of her uncle's money, he had not pressed his suit. There was Mrs. Vidal, and that really would be much better. A widow—and cash.

At the same moment Mrs. Vidal was reading the notice. She wondered if that was why she'd been able to make so little headway with Deschamps when she'd gone to the Embassy in connection with the release of her late husband's funds from France. Dorothy Vidal was used to making headway with men. She also wondered whether croissants for breakfast really put weight on you or not, then shrugged her shoulders and ate the croissant.

The three people most concerned did not see the notice at all in the morning. Howard Mantle, because he read *La Prensa;* Anne, because she went out early to ride; and Henri Deschamps because he read *La Nación*.

The Air France aircraft came in low over the suburban roof tops of Buenos Aires toward the airport of Moron. The passengers, their hands on their safety belts, ready to unfasten them as soon as they felt the bump of landing over, were already detached from each other and the casual intimacy of the trip.

The curious vacuum in which one exists during a voyage, in which one set of problems has been left behind and the need has not yet arisen to grapple with a new set, was over. Mme. Trinquard adjusted the little black felt hat on her dark hair and tried to see out. She liked traveling and she had never been in Buenos Aires before.

The plane made a neat landing, and automatically her fingers undid the belt. She wondered if Henri would be there to meet her and wondered again, as she had many times on the trip, about the girl he was going to marry. Henri was her brother and five years younger than she. A week before, she had received a cable to say that he was engaged and going to be married in a fortnight and could she come for the wedding. No information, except that the bride-to-be was an Anglo-Argentine, had been forthcoming. To Justine Trinquard it had seemed a little hurried, but she was reserving judgment. If Henri had finally got over the frail, lovely Geneviève, whose constitution had been unable to stand the rigors of the occupation, so much the better. The passengers were beginning to get up now, struggling with overcoats in the aisle. She followed the crowd out and toward the Immigration Office. Probably Henri would not be allowed in or out of some enclosure until she was through Immigration and Customs.

But Justine had reckoned without M. Mars. M. Mars was attached to the French Embassy in a rather vague capacity, but any errands connected with government offices were entrusted to him. By some mysterious means known only to himself, he always managed to accomplish them in about a quarter the time they would take anyone else. Henri Deschamps had, therefore, brought M. Mars to the airport with him.

M. Mars had left him seated in the Embassy car and said, "I have to speak to a friend." In a few minutes he returned. "We can remain here. My friend will let us know when the plane lands, and within five minutes we will have Mme. Trinquard all arranged."

Having listened to some tales of woe from people who'd come to the airport to meet friends and had three- or four-hour waits, Henri Deschamps was skeptical, but he had faith in M. Mars. He said, "I don't know whether it is your charm, or whether you know something with which to blackmail every member of this government."

"One has friends," said M. Mars. He was a round little man with a round head, like a tennis ball balanced on a football.

Henri nodded absent-mindedly. His sister was a highly efficient traveler. She'd done a lot of it and somehow always managed to arrive with baggage intact, keys, papers in order, and the minimum of fuss. He hoped she'd like Anne. Justine was all the close family he had now, since their father was dead. He tried to picture Anne through Justine's eyes and gave it up, and then through his father's eyes. What would the gentle, scholarly old invalid have made of her?

Justine would know. She had always known what their father would think or how he would feel about a given situation. It would be good to see Justine again. He'd hardly seen anything of her since the war—since the insane years after Geneviève had died. He didn't often think of them now; he'd taught himself not to. He wondered sometimes if Justine felt the same about Philippe Trinquard. Philippe had been killed only a week before the liberation of Paris. Justine had never mentioned that she was thinking of marrying again in her letters. But then she hardly ever wrote. In all fairness, he couldn't blame her for that, for neither did he. But he felt that, as she was a correspondent of a newspaper, she should write letters, whether he replied or not. "I have enough writing to do for the paper," she used to tell him, "besides, it runs in the family. Dad would cheerfully write a ten-thousand-word paper on the influence of Plato on modern French thought, but get him to send a postcard to say he's feeling all right! It can't be done."

Their father's slackness with correspondence had been a source of comfort to Henri, who did not write as a dutiful son should. He could always blame his father for not answering. "You wouldn't answer if I did write," he had defended himself.

"You've never tried it to find out," his father used to say. It all seemed so long ago.

A shirt-sleeved man came up to the car and said, "Passengers are coming off now." He led them through several doors marked PROHIBIDA LA ENTRADA, until they could see the line of people dribbling off the plane.

"Can you see Madame?" asked M. Mars.

"The tall woman in the gray tailleur with the gray overcoat and black hat," said Henri.

M. Mars was as good as his word. In little more than five minutes they were again in the car, Justine's passport duly stamped, her baggage passed unopened. M. Mars assured her what a pleasure it had been to be of assistance to her and tactfully got in front with the chauffeur.

On the way in to town they talked of nothing—of the trip—of Paris—of mutual friends. Henri explained when the road from the airport had been built. Unobtrusively they studied each other. They were curiously alike. They both had the same fine, clear-cut bone structure, the same black wavy hair, except that Henri took pains to keep his short cut. Lines, which his friends said were the result of war and his enemies credited to dissipation, made Henri look older than Justine, who had a quality that was not youth, but rather agelessness, in her face.

They arrived at the apartment block in Calle Sargento Cabral where Henri lived. "Actually got the place without paying key money from a fellow who worked in the Belgian Consulate and left in a hurry. Bought the furniture, of course, but I didn't have to pay more than it was worth. That's a miracle. It's worse here than Paris for apartments."

They thanked M. Mars again and went up. A maid came out and Henri said, "This is Dolores, who looks after me."

Dolores beamed from ear to ear, put out her hand and said, "*Mucho gusto, señora. Se parece mucho al señor!*"

"Do they always shake hands?" inquired Justine, going into the living room.

"In season and out. And they make personal remarks—like saying we were so much alike." Henri paused and added tentatively, "I suppose you want a bath and a rest."

She sensed an eagerness to talk going hand in hand with a certain nervousness. She said, "Later," and walked over to a desk which had a photograph on it.

For a while she studied the girl's picture. Large, wide-set eyes looked out at her: eyes which life had not shadowed, a face on which nothing was yet written.

"She's very pretty," she said at last.

"Her name's Anne Mantle. Her father had a jam factory here. Came out from Scotland with his brother as a very young man. Married a Campbell, born here. Both are dead.

Killed in a train wreck years ago. Anne's been brought up by her uncle—head of the Mantex Company. Frightfully rich. She's spent most of her time out of the country. School in Switzerland and later in the United States."

"So much for her family and financial suitability," said Justine with a faint smile. "Now tell me about her."

"You'll meet her tonight. We're dining at her uncle's house. She's not quite as tall as you——" Henri broke off. "You'll like her. She rides and plays tennis and golf."

"In spite of it, I'll like her, I expect," answered Justine, reflecting that he had told her nothing about the girl. "I hope so, if you love her."

"She's very, very attractive." Henri's eyes rested on the picture.

Justine recognized the tone in his voice, the speculative look in his eyes. It had been the precursor to various more or less violent affairs. But it hadn't been the tone of voice in which he'd spoken of Geneviève.

"What's the uncle like?"

"Fifty-five to sixty. Never married. All sorts of queer stories about him. He was supposed to have been in love with her mother. He's certainly devoted to Anne. He's also said to have murdered his partner about twenty-five years ago."

"Sounds charming."

"They never found out who did murder the partner. But the case against Mantle was 'Not Proven.' He turned into a hermit socially and made a fantastic fortune. It's only since Anne came home from college that he's started entertaining again, for her sake." Henri paused a moment and added, "He doesn't approve."

"Why not?"

"Probably thinks I'm after the money she'll have one day."

"You'll never make a fortune in the diplomatic service," observed Justine.

"The cash is an added attraction," admitted Henri. "As Dad used to say, 'Money is not necessary to a happy marriage, but I have never heard of it doing any harm.' There was an American Mantle approved of a bit more than me. Not that he approved of him very much. Stephen Sales. Decent fellow. Frightfully rich. Down here looking after his father's factory. He's crazy about Anne."

The telephone rang and Henri answered it. He turned back. "I have to go to the office. Be back for lunch. If you want anything, Dolores will know where it is. You'll have a bit of trouble getting used to the accent; they don't speak Spanish here. It's Argentine and almost a different language. But Dolores is very willing and quite bright."

For a long time after he had gone, she stood looking at the photograph of Anne Mantle. It all sounded very suitable and practical. The phone rang again. Justine picked it up.

"*Está el Señor Deschamps?*" asked a woman's voice. The Spanish had a foreign accent and the Deschamps was not said by a Frenchwoman.

"*No está,*" answered Justine. "*De la parte de quién?*"

"*Oh—er—dónde—cuando——*" It bogged down.

"*Vous parlez français?* You speak English? *Sprechen——*" began Justine hopefully.

"English," interrupted the voice. "Who's this speaking?"

"Mme. Trinquard. Henri's sister."

"Oh." The phone was hung up with a click. Justine stood

frowning at it for a moment, then lighted a cigarette and went into the bedroom.

"She does speak English," said Anne Mantle. She was fiddling with some glasses on the bar that occupied a corner of the big living room, and she had her back to her uncle.

"The advantages of an expensive schooling," mocked Howard Mantle. "Years of French in Switzerland and you stand there saying pathetically, 'She does speak English.'"

"There's a lot of difference between translating the works of Victor Hugo and talking to a gabbling Frenchwoman. They always rattle like machine guns," complained Anne, coming over to him.

"They probably think you rattle in English." He watched her, speculation on his worn gray face. "Stop fidgeting and sit down. They won't be here for another five minutes at least."

"I told Henri it didn't matter if she didn't have a long dress. I've no idea what she's brought, coming by plane. And she can't have much money, only what she earns on the paper. He said one time that her husband didn't leave anything. That's why I put this on." She pointed down to the long powder-blue jersey dress she wore, whose well-cut simplicity betrayed its price. "I didn't want her to feel— you know——"

"I know." Howard Mantle smiled and it completely altered his worn, hard face. "Stop fussing, will you? You're behaving like a schoolgirl instead of a twenty-five-year-old who told me she was a woman and knew how to run her life."

"I want her to like me."

"You're not marrying her. You're marrying Henri."

"But Justine's his only near relative, and if she didn't like me and you don't like Henri, it would all be rather dreary."

"I've told you, Anne, I don't dislike Henri. I don't think he's the right husband for you. We've been all through that."

"I know, and you've been an angel. But I still wish you did like him. All right, you do like him. But I wish you thought he was the right husband for me."

"I'm hoping he'll prove me wrong."

She stood in front of the big open fireplace. "I wonder if I should have gone to the plane with Henri today. I felt they hadn't seen each other for so long, and I am a stranger . . ." She paused for a moment, then went on. "I wonder if she's like Henri. I asked Louise Fareham about her yesterday. You know Henri had met the Farehams in Paris before the war. But Louise said she'd never even seen Justine."

Mantle, who had been watching her, said, "What?" suddenly.

"You haven't been listening to a word I said," she replied reproachfully.

"Sometimes you're uncannily like your mother——"

A car stopped on the road and then the bell from the garden gate rang. Mantle got up to go to meet his guests.

Dinner passed off smoothly. They were finishing their coffee when the sound of another car driving up made Anne look questioningly at her uncle. He said, "Canning said he might drop in on his way home from some *despedida* he was going to."

"This town is nothing but giving *despedidas* to people

who are going away and *bienvenidas* to them when they come back," Anne explained to Justine.

"Canning"—Mantle also turned to Justine to explain—"is fourth-generation Argentine. Used to be a crack athlete before the war. He went and fought with the British and lost a leg. Married an English girl while he was convalescing."

Right on top of the thumbnail sketch, Douglas Canning came in, walking with the slightly stiff caution dictated by the artificial leg. He greeted Anne and Mantle, then glanced at Henri and rather pointedly didn't shake hands with him. He said, "Didn't expect to find you here tonight."

Mantle looked sharply from one man to the other and introduced Canning to Justine. He bowed formally and moved to the chair Mantle pulled out from the fireplace for him.

"How's Gloria?" asked Anne.

"I seldom see her for long enough to inquire," Canning answered cheerfully. "She's gadding around the town somewhere tonight."

"Left you a grass widower, did she?" laughed Anne.

"I thought I knew where she was." Again Canning's eyes rested on Henri.

"What'll you drink, Douglas?" asked Mantle.

"Scotch and water, thanks."

"Is that what you're going to do as soon as we're married, Anne?" asked Henri. "Go gadding round the town and leave me a grass widower?"

"Depends how you behave," she told him.

"I knew I should marry an Argentine," said Henri with a mock sigh.

"Why?" inquired Justine.

"No genuine Argentine girl would suggest that her future husband's behavior could be anything but ideal," her brother answered.

"Probably because not so many Argentine girls marry Frenchmen," remarked Canning.

"How are you getting along witth your mother-in-law?" inquired Mantle hurriedly.

"Gloria's mother came out from England last week for a stay," Anne explained to Justine.

"The old girl's no bother. You'd hardly know she's in the house." Canning shifted to favor his leg. "Must do something about trotting her round."

"Bring her over for dinner," said Anne.

"Thanks, but she doesn't seem to be very socially minded."

"Is she going with you and Gloria to the Farehams' tomorrow night?" asked Anne. "You are going, aren't you?"

"We're going, and there's an argument raging over whether Gloria's mother should come. Gloria wants her to. I say she won't enjoy herself, and nobody consults the old girl."

The conversation went on like that: banal, meaningless, forced. After a little while Justine got up. "I hate to drag you away, Henri, but thirty-six hours of plane is quite tiring——" They said their good-bys.

Henri didn't talk on the way back into town, but when they reached the apartment he faced her and said, "Well?"

Justine smiled, the funny, wise little smile he knew so well. "She's charming. I like her."

"But . . . ?" he said when she paused.

"She's very young."

"She's twenty-five. Nine years younger than I."

"I wasn't thinking of years."

"Ah——" For some time he was silent, then he turned to her. For once his dark eyes were not laughing. He said flatly, with a kind of masochistic brutality, "She's as different from Geneviève as two women could be. So have they all been since."

She said, "I know."

"None of them have even remotely reminded me of her."

"Are you sure that Anne isn't—just another woman?"

He laughed. "Perhaps. But she's so full of verve. So divinely sure that it's a good world to live in, that everything is worth while. I adore it!"

"I hope you will a year hence," said Justine dryly. "Personally I'd find it a bit wearing as a steady diet."

"What did you think of Mantle?"

"A strange man," she said after a pause.

"Thought he looked ill tonight." Henri yawned.

She turned to go to her room. "Are you having any woman trouble?"

"One always has. They are so emotional. Why?"

"A woman called and asked for you, and when I said I was your sister, she hung up."

"Oh-oh. What did she talk?"

"Her Spanish was embryonic. English seemed to be her mother tongue."

A look of weary exasperation crossed his face. "Nothing I can't handle," he said. "Good night, Justine." He came over and kissed her. "It's wonderful to have you round again. You know what a scoundrel I am and you don't mind."

"One seldom loves people for their virtues. Probably why so many women have made fools of themselves over you. Good night."

Anne came over the following day with the car to take Justine out sight-seeing. They talked of the plans for the wedding, the invitations, of Anne's dress, and hardly noticed the Cathedral or the Casa Rosada. Finally Anne got around to talking of Henri. "I love his gaiety," she said.

"He said nearly the same thing about you."

"About me?" It seemed to surprise her. "You know, sometimes I realize how little I know about him. I mean, I've seen a lot of him and all that. But he never talks about himself."

"It's one of his good points," his sister admitted.

"But there's so much I want to know. About the war, for instance. I know men hate to talk about it, and I didn't see any of it and don't understand it. But if he'd tell me a bit, it would make me feel closer to him——" She broke off. "I'm explaining it very badly."

"I understand."

"Both sides in a marriage have got to understand to make a go of it. And he's not helping me to understand."

"Don't you realize that one of your greatest attractions for him is that you don't know anything about war and that you don't understand what it did to people?" asked Justine.

"That's rather a cruel thing to say," replied Anne.

"My dear, I didn't mean to be cruel," the older woman said quickly. "There's a great healing quality in forgetfulness. And forgetfulness does not come when you are with those who have shared the same experiences. You have so many things that Henri lacks. Faith in the future." With a crooked little smile she quoted his own words. "You are sure that the world is a good place to live in."

"If it isn't, it's our own fault for not making it so," retorted Anne.

"Perhaps you're right."

"Well!" The exclamation burst from Anne's lips. It was almost dark now, and they were driving back along Calle Cangallo. A taxi had turned into the driveway of a fairly large building which appeared to be a private house. For a second passing headlights had shown a redheaded woman in the corner. "Gloria Canning! I wonder who was with her?"

"Is Gloria Canning the wife of the man I met last night?" asked Justine, and didn't say that she had recognized Henri in the cab.

"Yes—and that house——" Anne leaned forward and said to the chauffeur, "Domingo, that house with the driveway that we passed, where the car was going in—what is it?"

"I believe it is an *amueblado, señorita*," the man answered vaguely.

"I'm sure that's the house Uncle pointed out to me one time. He said it was a very famous—you know——" She stopped and after a minute said, "Damn! That's foul."

"What?"

"Douglas Canning's such a pet. He was a wonderful amateur boxer before the war, they say. And then he lost his leg. Way above the knee, I believe. And he has a lot of pain from it."

Justine's face was enigmatical in the gathering dark. "So you think his wife should be faithful to him because he has a lot of pain."

"Now you're laughing at me! I know Uncle once said she married him in—now what was it? A miasma of sentimentalism which she mistook for patriotism, and pity which she mistook for love, with a good many illusions about South America thrown in."

"Perhaps it wasn't she," said Justine carelessly.

"I'd know her hair anywhere. It's lovely and not a scrap touched up. She's a marvelous-looking creature." Anne said it with frank admiration. "All the women want to scratch her eyes out."

They were turning into Sargento Cabral, and Anne said, "I'll be seeing you at eight-thirty at the Farehams'."

Justine thanked her for the drive and went on up to the apartment. Henri was not in. She thought of Canning's words last night: "Didn't expect to find you here tonight" and "I thought I knew where she was." Justine put two and two together and, oddly enough, made four.

CHAPTER 2

"Oh, but you must come!" Louise Fareham held the telephone with one hand while she tried to fasten a suspender with the other. "I mean, we'd be so disappointed not to have you, and we'd be thirteen without you." There was a pause during which she listened, got the suspender done, and started arranging the shoulder strap of her slip. "I'm sure we won't sit down till late. Probably ten. Somehow one never manages to here. Couldn't you make it by then? If we're thirteen, the soufflé will be ruined, someone will develop acute indigestion, and probably the roof will give way. Try. Please. Okay. Get back to your conference or meeting or whatever it is and tell them you've got a union that won't allow you to work any later. Stop them telling rude stories and keep them to business. You remember where we are, don't you? Seventeenth floor." She put down the telephone.

Her husband called from his bedroom, "That's what comes of asking fourteen. Who was that?"

"Rick Vanner. You know, the visiting fireman."

"I don't know why you have so many," Robert Fareham complained. "Ten's all right. Twelve's uncomfortable, and fourteen is like the subway at rush hour. Somebody's usually sitting halfway into the living room."

"That'll be you, darling. I'm putting the Frenchwoman next to you, and Howard Mantle and I will sit at the other end. That's the only way to do it."

"Deschamps' sister? Does she speak English or Spanish?"

"Don't ask me. Didn't you meet her in Paris?"

"No. Only met him."

"I thought you did that night you went to that play when I couldn't go."

"No." Fareham was making faces at the mirror in his endeavors to make his tie behave. He wandered into Louise's room. The light on her mirror was better.

"I'll have to put Steve Sales at the other end of the table from Henri or he'll probably put poison in his soup or something. Where's my—— Here it is." She applied mascara for a minute in silence. "I was so sure Steve and Anne——"

"Who else have you got coming? The Cannings?"

"And Arrietti. I'd asked him before I knew I was going to have too many men. Michel Fresne. I thought in case the sister only speaks French, he'd be handy. Fred Elting. He's a grass widower these days."

"Did his wife go already?"

"Last week. Don't you remember I told you the Trent woman said she thought she wouldn't come back, either? That she'd probably get a divorce in the States."

"Uhuh. I remember." Robert Fareham surveyed himself in the mirror with considerable disapproval. He was only fifty-eight, but on occasions when his wife had a dinner party he felt ninety-eight.

"Bob, are you dressed? Go and see Josefina isn't doing anything mad with the wine and find out if the other girls have come yet."

"Is Jorge coming to look after the drinks?"

"I couldn't get him. I've the three extra girls coming, and you'll have to be barman."

"Why don't we live on a mountaintop with no neighbors? Though I must say it suits you. You're looking very pretty."

"Liar. I'm only half made-up yet."

"I like you better without it." He dropped a kiss on the top of her head and went out to superintend the wines.

At about a quarter to nine the first guests began to arrive, and by nine-thirty several cocktails had circulated and conversation was normal: it was ranging from labor troubles, the slump in the peso, the rise in prices, through to the latest stories about Peron and Evita.

Steve Sales had greeted Henri Deschamps in quite a civilized manner. Michel Fresne, his services as interpreter not being needed, was paying attention to Dorothy Vidal, who was recounting something extraordinary that had happened to her. She was one of those people who seem unable to go down the street to mail a letter without encountering some strange drama. Her face was alight and vivacious now, as she talked. It was, whenever she talked to a man, thought Louise, and wondered if Dorothy really wanted to marry again. Vidal had left her plenty of money and she always had men on the string. Louise's eyes passed to the Cannings.

They weren't fighting tonight, which was a comfort. Sometimes their marital differences became embarrassing.

Louise looked over her other guests. Dr. Arrietti, the only hundred-per-cent Argentine present, was talking French to Mme. Trinquard. Fred Elting was helping Bob with the drinks. Henri Deschamps was talking to his fiancée while her uncle watched with a curious expression on his drawn gray face.

Everything was all right so far. Now if only the visiting fireman would arrive. She must ask Bob before he came whether to introduce him as Commander Vanner or Mr. Vanner. She never remembered. He was out of the navy now, she gathered. She heard the front doorbell ring and heaved a sigh of relief as she saw a tall figure appear and look round for her. At least they wouldn't be thirteen.

"You really are frightfully noble to come," Louise greeted Richard Vanner. "You should get an extra medal or a front seat in heaven or something."

"I didn't want to miss the party." Rick Vanner lied like a gentleman. "But when I saw it getting later and later——" He broke off with an expressive shrug. "I must apologize for being dirty. I came straight from the meeting."

"Doesn't matter. You're here. You see, it was too late to find anyone else or put anyone off. I was wondering whether to disappear suddenly and say I felt an epileptic fit coming on, so that there'd be twelve, but that would be so embarrassing for Bob. Then I thought I'd take my plate out and sit in the living room." Louise rattled along with her cheerful nonsense. "And I meant to ask Bob. He always knows these things and I never do, and then I forgot."

31

Not being clairvoyant, Rick Vanner looked a trifle bewildered. He said, "Anything I might know?"

"Of course. It's about you. Do I introduce you as Commander or Mr.?"

"No rank, please. I'm out of the navy now—until World War III gets started."

"Don't say things like that! I've a horrible feeling that saying it makes it come nearer. Come and be introduced." She led him round the room. All the guests were strangers to Vanner, except Howard Mantle, whom he'd interviewed once in his office, and Steve Sales. Fareham gave him one of the largest and strongest drinks he'd ever had, with the explanation, "You're behind."

They went in to dinner.

"I've put cards," Louise said. "Can you find yourselves? This isn't a seating arrangement. It's an effort to split up the women."

Rick found himself on the left of his hostess, with Steve Sales on his left. "Steve was telling us all sorts of exciting things about you, Mr. Vanner," said Louise, "but now he says you've left Naval Intelligence."

"Private enterprise pays better," Rick told her.

"But is it so exciting?"

"No, thank God," he answered fervently.

Louise laughed. "But what exactly do you call yourself? I tried to explain to someone the other day and I couldn't. Are you a detective?"

"More or less. My office door says 'Investigations,'" explained Rick. "I specialize in foreign inquiries. If some firm wants to know why they are having trouble in a given country and they are ready to pay my fees and expenses, I'll go and find out for them."

"Trouble shooter," supplied Steve Sales.

"Yes, but investigator sounds more dignified. I can charge bigger fees."

"How are you coming along here?" asked Steve.

"Finished. I'm leaving tomorrow if I can find an aircraft."

"What a shame! Bob and I'd hoped you'd be staying around Buenos Aires for a bit." Louise turned to listen to something Howard Mantle, seated at her right, was saying.

Somebody was talking about an amateur performance of *Blithe Spirit* which was going to be given the following night.

"Who is playing the man with the ghost wife?" asked Bob.

"Hugh Blake, and if he ever knows his lines it's going to be a miracle," said Gloria Canning.

"Are you the ghost wife or the other?" asked Fred Elting.

"The ghost. Elvira," Gloria told him. "I'm having the most frightful time with the make-up. It's a sort of weird gray. But it's got to look attractive at the same time as ghostly."

"Ghostly or ghastly?" asked her husband.

"It needs a face with a good bone structure," said Dorothy Vidal.

"That's what Mrs. Rockwell said when she asked me to play the part," answered Gloria sweetly.

"I told Mrs. Rockwell that after the *hell* I went through with *The Circle*, I couldn't *face* another," said Dorothy. "I'll never forget that performance as long as I live."

"The high spot to me," put in Sales, "was when the

siphon backfired when what's-his-name got a whisky and soda at a tense moment, and made the most obscene noises."

Dorothy Vidal waited until the general laugh of recollection had died down and then continued. "I had the most awful grippe, and I'd had some very upsetting news . . ." She paused, her face momentarily shadowed.

Canning murmured sotto voce to Fareham, "Got a record of *Pagliacci?*" and Bob glared at him.

"I got out of bed to go to the theater, with a temperature of 104," continued Dorothy. "My throat was *agony* every line I said. I collapsed when it was over."

"Very gracefully, I remember," remarked Canning dryly, "into Carter's arms."

"You should never have got up from bed," said Michel Fresne.

Dorothy flashed him a smile down the length of the table. "They were depending on me," she said.

Vanner thought he detected a faint amusement on the face of Dr. Arrietti, who was seated next to Mrs. Vidal. Louise was asking him if he'd ever done any theatricals and he shook his head.

"I don't know who enjoys them," she said. "The people who act in them always seem to be in a dither of nerves and the audience in an abyss of boredom. If you're still here tomorrow night, you'll have to go."

"And be bored?"

"Do your duty by your country," Louise told him, looking round the table. Conversation was general again. Someone was talking about the fight. It was the night of the Joe Louis-Joe Walcott fight. "We'll be able to get it on the radio," she said.

Sales and Mantle were talking across the corner of the table about a lawsuit upcountry. "Comes up next week," Mantle was saying. "If I've time, I'll go up. But I've got it pretty well fixed."

"Got the judge in your pocket?" inquired Dorothy.

"Have to if you're going to get justice round here," answered Mantle.

"Depends on your definition of justice," remarked Dr. Arrietti.

"There's no question about it. We're in the right." Mantle practically dismissed the subject.

"But you evidently don't want to take a chance on the judge disagreeing with you," put in Rick, who felt it was time he contributed to the conversation.

"You're not drinking any wine," Louise interrupted a bit hurriedly.

"Not with my doctor looking," Mantle told her, and then replied to Rick. "If you don't make your own justice, there won't be any."

"Dangerous theory," replied Rick.

"Probably doesn't make much difference," said Louise. "The people are going to feel they've been cheated anyway. I've never heard of a lawsuit where the parties concerned thought they got justice."

"Perhaps there's never been one," suggested Sales.

"What about Solomon?" asked Rick.

"D'you think the people who actually received his judgments approved? They probably squawked as hard as any ambulance chaser whose motion for a million dollars of damages was denied," said Louise.

They started talking about the growth of the ambulance-

35

chasing racket in Buenos Aires. Rick studied his fellow guests. Was it his imagination or was everybody making very marked and not too successful efforts to be gay? There seemed to be a febrile, forced note.

Louise sensed it too. But as long as everything went smoothly, she didn't mind. She glanced at her watch as they got up from the table. Eleven-fifteen. That was all right. With a bit of luck they might all be gone by one. Bob turned on the radio. The fight had started.

It was half an hour later that Douglas Canning made his way along the passage to Bob Fareham's bedroom. In the doorway he stopped. After a second's silence he said, "Good God!"

Stephen Sales was on his knees beside the fallen figure of Henri Deschamps, who lay half in and half out of the door to the bathroom, his head a few inches from the base of the washbowl. On the bath mat was an empty glass, not broken. In Sales's hand was what appeared to be a dagger.

To be accurate, it was a Bolivian poncho pin, about nine inches long and sharply pointed. At the top was a silver ball, about three inches in diameter. The pin went through the ball and terminated in a ring to which was attached a cross, more or less Maltese in shape. The cross had dropped against Sales's hand and blood dripped from the end of the pin.

There was confusion. Dr. Arrietti came and said that Deschamps was dead. Canning returned to a seat convenient to the bar. Rick Vanner watched them, half his mind revolving the problem, the other half cursing himself. Why hadn't he been firm and told Louise Fareham that, thirteen or not at table, he couldn't come to dinner? Why did he have to get mixed up in a murder?

Justine Trinquard went slowly into the bedroom and stood looking down at the body. She knelt, laid her hand for a minute on the black hair, disordered now and curly and showing streaks of gray, though Henri had been only thirty-four. She didn't cry. She got up at last and went back into the living room. Louise Fareham had told Anne, who was sobbing quietly. Justine sat beside her and put an arm round her.

"Justine, you can't just stop someone like Henri! You can't——" Anne lifted a wet face, her blue eyes holding the instinctive revolt of youth against the things that are.

The older woman looked down at her and a fleeting smile crossed her face; it was an infinitely tired and sad little smile that revealed for a second all the weary knowledge, the dull, hopeless resignation of a tired and broken continent.

Vanner shook himself to free himself from the pictures it brought to his mind. Sometimes he wondered why he'd picked an occupation which, by its very nature, pitchforked him into the vortices of violence and misery of the world. If only he'd been a soda clerk in some smugly progressive and prosperous small town, there'd be so many things that he would never have seen or known, pictures of tragedy and suffering which sometimes stalked through his mind like phantasms of a nightmare. It must be admitted that Rick didn't spend a great deal of time worrying over the woes of the world; he was an exceptionally practical man and knew that his worrying over them wasn't going to help anyone. But one couldn't help being aware of them sometimes. And he had not expected to run into violence tonight.

Canning was moving, preparatory to getting up for another drink. Rick saw the momentary pain between his eyebrows. More wreckage of war, he supposed, without knowing the man's history. He said, "What are you drinking and I'll get it."

Mrs. Vidal detached herself from Michel Fresne, who was hovering around her protectively, saying, "Are you sure you're all right?"

She nodded, making a dramatic effort to pull herself together. "One can't help remembering, sometimes," she said, apropos of what, no one knew.

Fred Elting was looking at the silenced radio. "I wonder who did win," he said.

Gloria Canning said, "What?"

"The fight."

"How can you think about the fight?" she demanded with a brittle note under her voice.

Bob Fareham came back into the room and said, "I've called the police."

"But surely we don't have to have the Argentine police?" said Dorothy.

"What d'you think we should have, the Chinese?" asked Elting.

"But we're all British or American," began Gloria.

"You have the strangest ideas of the privileges of the British abroad," her husband said acidly. "I might also draw your attention to the fact that we are not all British and American. The corpse was French——"

"Sh," said Fareham, with an anxious glance toward Justine and Anne.

"His sister, the nearest of kin, is French," went on Canning imperturbably. "Arrietti is Argentino and so am I——"

"You! But you're——" began Gloria.

"I'm Argentine and don't forget it."

"You've been drinking too much," she snapped.

"Not nearly enough, my dear."

"Where's Howard?" said Louise suddenly.

Everyone looked round rather as if Howard Mantle was likely to be concealed in an ash tray or under a chair. Nobody had seen him for some time.

Vanner had seen Mantle go down the passage. There appeared to be three bedrooms, as far as he could judge from the doors. He handed Canning his drink and picked up the one he had poured for himself. It was improbable that Mantle would be in the bedroom the women were using for their wraps. He was not in the room with the corpse. The door of the third room was closed. Rick opened it and went in. It turned out to be a study, lined with bookshelves. On a couch at the far side lay Howard Mantle. He turned his head as Vanner came in but otherwise didn't move. Rick went over and stood beside him, looking down at the gray, pain-drawn face.

"Don't say anything to the others," said Mantle. "I don't want a fuss."

"Heart?"

Mantle nodded. "I heard a disturbance. What happened?"

"How bad is it?" Rick ignored his question.

Mantle sat up. "Anne——"

"She's all right." Wishing he'd brought the doctor, Rick assessed the strong face with its deep lines of tragedy and spoke accordingly. "Henri Deschamps has been murdered."

39

"I must go to Anne." Mantle asked no questions and showed no interest in the killing. "Help me up."

"Hadn't you better——" began Rick.

"I'll be all right." Once on his feet, Mantle walked steadily toward the door. For a moment he turned. "She doesn't know anything about this business." He went on out.

CHAPTER 3

An *agente* arrived, which is the ordinary policeman from the corner. He looked at the corpse, looked at the guests, spoke to Arrietti and Fareham, looked worried and went to the telephone. The *comisario* arrived next, the chief of the *comisaría seccional*, or local police station. He brought numbers of men in his train. Among them were the *señor auxiliar*, his chief helper, the *oficial escribiente*, or clerk, and several other grades of police officers. They seemed to take up a great deal of space in the apartment and to get considerably in one another's way.

The *comisario* looked worried when he arrived. He wished, he said, to make the *inspección ocular*. He also looked at the corpse and the guests, spoke to the *agente*, and then used the telephone. When that was done he asked to see everyone's *documentos*.

Mrs. Vidal didn't have hers, nor did Gloria Canning. The official obviously thought there was something peculiar and more than a little suspicious about people who didn't carry

either a *cédula* or passport with them. He said so. It took
him some time before the *oficial escribiente* had entered
everyone's name, address, business and civil status, together
with passport or *cédula* number, in the book he produced.
By the time that was finished, the police doctor arrived.

He confirmed what everyone already knew. That Henri
Deschamps was dead and that the cause of death was two
wounds inflicted in his back by the Bolivian poncho pin.

"They were struck, it appears," said the doctor, "with
considerable force and an accurate knowledge of anatomy."

"Could it have been done by a woman?" asked the *comisario*.

"By a strong woman—or a woman in a passion of rage—
yes," said the doctor. "This pin is as strong as a dagger and
much more pointed and sharp than most."

"You're not fooling anyone!" Fred Elting's voice carried
a sneering inflection to Rick Vanner's ears, and he looked
round to the little bar where Elting had been helping himself to liquid refreshment since dinner. Steve Sales was con-
fronting him, his eyes hard, a little white line round his
mouth.

"Suppose you say what you mean." Sales hardly more
than whispered the words.

"We all know you're ready to break out the champagne
in celebration," sneered Elting. "You've a clear field again."

Rick Vanner looked—and was—lazy, but he could move
remarkably fast when he chose. He chose now. One stride
took him to Sales. As the latter swung, Rick interposed his
solid shoulder between the two men, at the same time strik-
ing down Sales's arm.

"Keep out of this," snapped Sales, his face white and set.

"Not the time or the place, boys," Rick said, quite casually, but his hold on Sales's arm was paralyzing. He felt Sales's muscles relax and in turn relaxed his own hold.

"No, you're right." Steve spoke with an effort, as if he'd been running hard. "There will be—later."

Vanner frowned. If ever he'd seen murder in a man's eyes, it had been in Stephen Sales's then.

"Of course a general massacre would be fun," said Canning, who had remained seated near the bar, watching everything with a half-somnolent, half-malicious amusement.

"Once a policeman, always a policeman," Elting said to Vanner.

Rick looked him over with some distaste. His eyes traveled up and down the flabby frame under a dark suit with too loud a pin stripe; he took in the pouches under the eyes, the looseness of the mouth. "Rather lucky for you," he said.

Elting's mouth twitched with anger. "Seems to me one's back needs watching round here," he retorted.

The reappearance of the *comisario* from the bedroom, accompanied by some of his numerous assistants, was opportune. The *comisario* regretted, politely, but he had to ask some questions. Would everyone be seated?

He had to establish when last the dead man had been seen alive. They had come out from dinner, he understood, at eleven-fifteen. Where had they gone? It took him half an hour to sort out the volunteered information, which was vague and inconclusive. The women had been in and out of Louise's bedroom and bathroom. Some of the men had used the bathroom in Bob's room. The radio had been turned on for the fight. It had been quite loud, as the static

43

interruption seemed worse when it was tuned down. People had changed seats in order to be farther from it or nearer to it, as their tastes dictated. People had gone across to the bar to talk to Bob or to get a drink.

"From the preliminary medical examination," said the *comisario* stiffly, "it would appear that the deceased had been dead about five minutes when he was found. When was that?"

There was a confusion of voices, all saying "about" some time or other. When they had died down, Vanner said flatly, "It was eleven forty-seven."

The *comisario* looked relieved. "You are sure, señor?"

"It was eleven forty-seven," amended Rick precisely, "when Mr. Canning exclaimed 'Good God!' "

"And you said that you had—found—the body less than a minute before, Señor Sales?"

"Yes."

"You were going to the bathroom. What did you do, exactly, please?"

"I saw him from the bedroom door. I thought he'd had an accident, been taken ill; I don't know exactly what I did think," admitted Steve. "I knew he wasn't drunk, or rather, that he had not been the last time I'd noticed him. So I went over and found that he was dead."

"Why did you pull out the dagger?"

"I was going to turn him over to see if there was anything that could be done."

"You weren't sure he was dead?"

"Not sure—no. I thought he was." Sales's mouth twisted a little. "My experience runs more to gunshot and high-explosive wounds than to stabbing in the back."

"But Señor Canning came to the door before you turned him over?"

"Yes."

"Why didn't you call the doctor? There was a doctor here."

"Perfectly honestly, I didn't think."

"And, finally, you never did turn him over."

"When I got a good look at his face, I realized——" Sales cast a worried look at Anne and stopped. "In a war one gets to recognize death," he ended simply.

"How long had you known the deceased?"

"About a year. Since he came down here from Brazil."

"Had you ever quarreled with him?"

"No."

"Now I'll tell one," said Mrs. Vidal in English.

The *comisario* looked up at the interruption. He did not understand English, but the tone of her voice was unmistakable. "The señora does not agree?"

At that instant a soft but unmistakable snore came from Douglas Canning. Vanner, who was near him, touched his shoulder lightly and he opened his eyes. "Sorry," he said.

"You're drunk," said Gloria disgustedly.

"You have," replied her husband, "a genius for stating the obvious."

Rick was considering Canning thoughtfully. The man had been drinking a good deal and he undoubtedly had fallen asleep. Somehow Rick didn't think he was drunk.

The *comisario* went back to the question of exactly what people had done after they had come out from the dining room. As was to be expected, the answers were vague and contradictory. On only one subject was there unanimity.

45

That Bob Fareham had gone straight to the radio and tuned it in on the fight. Everyone said that he or she had "drifted around," "talked to different people" but could not remember who or in what order. They had also "listened to the fight" and gone to one or other of the bedrooms.

Considering the small passage that led from the arch of the living room toward the two bedrooms and the study, and the number of people who made trips there, it was phenomenal how they all seemed to have gone back and forth without seeing any of the others. Definitely phenomenal, thought Rick. As the questioning wore on he found it harder and harder to believe. There had, of course, been quite a lot of drinking before dinner, and there had been two wines with dinner, and drinks were circulating again before Deschamps met his death. But still it was amazing how little people had noticed.

From his own memory, Rick checked what was said. He himself had not paid a great deal of attention to his fellow guests. The fight had interested him more. He liked the Farehams and he'd liked what he'd known of Sales, but the other people he was not likely to meet again and he hadn't put himself out to any degree to notice them. It was a pity he had seated himself in the corner by the radio, for it had not been a good spot from which to observe the comings and goings in the room. But then how in God's name was he to know that somebody was going to get himself murdered?

With infinite patience, the official was compiling a schedule. He started it on several dozen different sheets of paper and it invariably had to be amended. When it was compiled it was remarkable in that it suggested that the murdered man had rendered himself invisible for ten or more minutes. He had spoken to Anne and to his sister, and Elting had spoken to him shortly after they had all come in from the dining room, and from that time on he had disappeared until his body was found.

There were a lot of things that didn't quite jell. They irritated Rick's professional mind. He couldn't decide how much the witnesses were vague and forgetful, how much they were deliberately lying to protect either themselves or someone else, or whether they just shrank from getting anyone else in trouble.

The *comisario* was going on now to the question of the Bolivian poncho pin. Everyone in the room, with the exception of Justine, admitted having seen the dagger many times and knowing that it was always among a number of other Bolivian and Peruvian antiquities on the top of the bookshelves between the little bar and the radio.

"I remember one time telling Louise it would be a wonderful weapon for a murder," said Dorothy Vidal, looking very dramatic. Rick waited for her to say, "If we'd only known," or that she had had a premonition. She said neither and he was disappointed.

When it came to establishing when anybody had last noticed the pin on the shelf, the official wasn't so lucky. Before dinner, people had stood by the bookshelves and leaned against them while they talked to Bob, who was mixing drinks, but they had not been looking at the ornaments. Finally, in despair, he appealed to Bob. "Señor Fareham, don't you know? It is your house. Didn't you notice if it was still there?"

"Really, you know, one doesn't go round checking the

portable objects to see they haven't disappeared," Bob told him. "Wouldn't look polite."

The *comisario* looked reproachful and asked, almost pathetically, if someone hadn't seen it since dinner.

"Señor Elting, you were standing at this end of the radio?"

"It's like Bob Fareham says, you're not watching to see if someone pinches something," said Elting.

Thinking back, it seemed to Rick that almost everybody had at some time or another stood near the shelf. It was a convenient place to stand to talk to Bob, to get a drink, to bring back an empty glass. At one time or another he had noticed Arrietti there, Fresne, Mantle, Sales, and Elting before the last-named had moved to his vantage point at the end of the shelf by the radio.

One thing the *comisario* didn't mention was the empty glass on the bath mat. It interested Rick. It seemed odd, somehow, that if Deschamps had finished his drink he would not have put the glass down somewhere. People don't usually carry an empty glass around with them at parties, except to replace it on a bar. It was a pity that the glass had had a knitted sock round it, he thought; the fingerprints might have been useful.

The *comisario* was looking none too happily at the two schedules he had composed and decided to give them up for the time being. "Do any of you know of any enemies of M. Deschamps?" he asked.

More than half the eyes in the room turned to Steve Sales. His face tautened and his mouth set, but he said nothing.

"Señor Fareham?"

"Don't know of any," said Bob flatly.

"Nor I," said Louise when the *comisario's* eyes rested on her.

Arrietti shook his head. "No, but I did not know him well."

"Señora Vidal?"

"One does not wish to make accusations."

"Señor Fresne? You are a fellow countryman of his."

Fresne tugged at his upper lip as if he expected to find a mustache there and said, "I met him for the first time tonight."

Elting, when it came to his turn, looked at Steve, but he said, "You'll probably find some husband around the town that doesn't love him."

Justine looked across at him suddenly and her eyes were hard.

Gloria Canning said, in English, "It isn't husbands that I'd look for."

Howard Mantle answered frankly, "I haven't heard of any."

Vanner said, "I only met him tonight," and the *comisario* looked disappointed.

"Mme. Trinquard," he said, "you are his sister. Do you not know of any?"

"In France, yes," she said slowly, "but here in Buenos Aires, I know of none."

Dr. Arrietti had been watching Mantle and looking increasingly worried for the past hour. Now he rose from his seat and went and spoke to the *comisario* in a low voice. The official nodded and a few minutes later he said, "There will be a diligent investigation into all the circumstances

49

of this crime. You will hold yourself at the disposal of the police for further questioning. *Buenas noches, señores y señoras.*"

Everybody started to talk at once, and above them all Mrs. Vidal's voice rose. "But aren't they going to arrest him?"

"Who?" asked Fareham with a harassed absent-mindedness.

"It must be obvious!" she snorted.

"Well, they say in the States you can't hang a million dollars," Fred Elting was remarking to Fresne, and his eyes were on Sales as he spoke.

"But you must come back and spend the night with us." Mantle spoke to Justine.

"You can't go to that apartment alone." Anne added her word.

"If you'd rather stay here"—Louise had joined them—"we have a bedroom."

"Please, it's very kind of you all. But I would prefer to go back to the apartment." A taut note in Justine's voice warned that the control she had maintained would not last much longer.

"Anne——" Steve came over. "You know—I mean—if there is anything I can do——"

Anne gave him a watery smile, and then Gloria Canning's voice cut across. "That is a bit raw!" Sales's face whitened and the grim misery sank deeper in it. For the first time Anne realized. She held out her hand to him and said, "Thanks, Steve. I know you'd——" but she couldn't get any further.

Mantle said, "Let's go home, my dear."

"Come on, Gloria," Canning was saying.

"Where are my gloves?"

"I've got them in my pocket. Come along." Canning's voice held the irritation of nerves and fatigue.

Down below on the sidewalk Mantle and Anne, accompanied by the doctor, were standing by their car. They were going to drive Justine home. Some kind of discussion was going on between Fresne and Elting as to which should take Dorothy Vidal home. She lived only half a block away. She finally settled it by saying, "Both of you come and have a drink with me. My nerves are in shreds."

Sales, who had just come out, made an instinctive movement toward Elting. Vanner, who had ridden down in the same elevator load with him, called out sharply, "Sales!"

Michel Fresne had Dorothy Vidal's right arm; Elting hurriedly took her left.

Rick caught up with Sales. "Still isn't the time or the place. Come up to my room. I've a bottle there." He was staying in the Plaza Hotel, less than half a block away.

"Sure you don't mind being seen with a convicted murderer?" asked Steve bitterly.

CHAPTER 4

Vanner didn't say anything until they had reached his room and he'd produced a bottle of whisky from his suitcase. "I'll see if I can get any ice sent up."

"Not on my account," said Steve. "I'll settle for it straight and warm."

They did. Rick considered what he knew of Stephen Sales. It was not a great deal. His father had made a vast fortune out of some kind of sauce for seasoning. When the war had come, Steve had gone into the navy. Having known a good deal about yachts, he'd eventually become commander of a submarine. He and his submarine had been put under Vanner's orders for a job in the Aleutian Islands. It had been at the end of a long, dangerous assignment when Rick had been ill, exhausted and with every nerve strained to breaking point. He remembered the elderly captain at the base who had listened to his request for a submarine. "Intelligence men! You're all mad," he had growled, looking at the orders Vanner had given him. "You're not fit for anything but sick bay, but I suppose I've got to give you what you want. I'll give you Sales—God help him."

Looking back on it, Rick decided that Sales must often have needed God's help. He must have been anything but a reasonable superior to the young lieutenant. He didn't remember much about it all now, except that he'd finished the job he'd been sent to do. He probably owed Sales apologies, but the younger man had seemed genuinely pleased to see him when they'd met again the week before.

"Pretty good way to know who your friends are," Sales was saying. "Get accused of murder."

"You haven't been accused yet."

"They'll do that in the morning." Steve finished his drink and Rick filled up the tooth glass again. "I didn't kill him, you know." Rick was silent for a moment, replenishing his own drink. "You don't believe me."

"It was dumb of you to touch the dagger," said Rick.

"I know. But I only thought of that when I saw it written largely in everyone's face that they thought I'd done it. Believe it or not, when I saw Deschamps there on the floor, my first idea was to help him."

"If you didn't kill him, who did?"

"Haven't you got the answer?" Steve looked up with a half-smile. "You always had the answer for everything in the Aleutians."

"I don't remember a hell of a lot about that assignment," confessed Rick. "Was I a complete swine?"

Sales shook his head. "You were the most icily polite superior I'd ever had—and the least human. One of the men said one time, 'Ain't the weather cold enough up here without that human iceberg?' We didn't realize until the end how completely bushed you were."

"I don't remember getting back."

"I sent you ashore on a stretcher when we got in. When the job was finished, you just folded up. It's the only way I can describe it. You gave me the last orders, perfectly clearly and impersonally, as if I were a dictaphone, about the prisoners. A minute later I turned to tell you something and you were out cold."

"I was tired."

"I heard something about that assignment of yours after. It must have been hell."

"I was scared as hell the whole time and I didn't like it," said Rick. "Tell me about these people who were at the dinner tonight. D'you know them all well?"

"Most of them. Deschamps' sister I'd never met before. Arrietti, the doctor, is a very old friend of Mantle's and I've often met him at their house. One sees Mrs. Vidal round everywhere, but I don't know her well. Ditto Michel Fresne. The Farehams I've known ever since I came down. They're swell people. I see quite a bit of the Cannings. Elting . . ." Sales paused and his face hardened. "Elting has never liked me or I him. When we put up the factory originally, before I was down here, he tried to hold us up on some land. Chester, our man in charge, was a fairly tough egg, and Elting didn't get away with it. But he's got pals in the government, and every time we want anything, permits and so on, he does his damnedest to block 'em."

"Vindictive sort of person. Hm. Would he have any reason for wanting to murder Deschamps?"

"Not that I know of," said Sales, and added with a wry smile, "unfortunately. Why?"

"If you didn't do it, somebody else did. I'm paging candidates."

"I suppose it was done by somebody who was at dinner. I mean, it couldn't have been someone from outside?"

"Someone who came up in the elevator, got in through the front door, which has a spring lock, without being observed, came into the living room and took the Bolivian pin, also without being observed, went to the bedroom, killed Deschamps, and left, still without being observed?" Rich raised one eyebrow. "Or someone who came up in the service elevator, which I understand is at the back of the kitchen. The kitchen can't be very large, to go by the plan of the place. So the murderer got through the kitchen, where there were four maids around, got through the service door to the living room, stole the dagger, et cetera, as before and, also as before, all quite unnoticed."

"People are unobservant," said Sales.

"Granted. But that's asking them to be completely blind. Also, my dear fellow, if you're setting out to murder a man, you usually go equipped with a weapon. You don't leave it to chance to find one."

Steve nodded. "But I don't see who——" he began.

"What d'you know about Deschamps?"

"He came here from Rio. He'd been in the French Embassy there. That was about a year ago. I met him originally through the French naval attaché. I used often to see him at cocktail parties and dinners. He was an unattached male, which is useful to hostesses, and he was amusing. At least, he was as a rule. Tonight he hardly said a thing. I some-times thought——" He stopped.

"What?"

"Nothing. Just an impression. I felt his gaiety might have been an act. It was, in a way, more a defense." Steve stopped again and gave a short laugh. "I'm no good at explaining that sort of thing."

"Go on and try to forget the '*de mortuis*' and that a little gentleman doesn't say anything against the guy his girl decides to marry," suggested Rick. "Tell me what you thought about him."

Steve got up and ranged round the room. "All the women ran after him. And there was always gossip. Hell, I'm not criticizing him for that. Lord knows, I'm not a plaster saint."

"Single women or married ones?" asked Rick.

"Married, as a rule."

Vanner's mind canvassed the married couples. Louise Fareham seemed improbable. He said, "Such as Gloria Canning?"

"You've heard the story too?" Steve refilled his glass.

"What d'you know about Mantle?"

"He's rich as Croesus. He doesn't much like me."

"Why not?"

"Probably because he knows I want to marry Anne."

"Anne will be wealthy," remarked Rick.

"Yes. Mantle was against the marriage." Steve smiled wryly. "Anne told me. She said it was the one thing that was making her unhappy. I asked what he had against Des-champs, and she said he simply didn't think that Henri was the man for her. Anne knew the stories about him."

"Mantle disapproved but finally gave his consent?"

"Yes."

"And he's the man who is said to have murdered his partner."

"Oh, hundreds of years ago. I've heard that tale. It was 'Not Proven.'" Steve suddenly sat down. "But, good God, he wouldn't——"

"He has some kind of heart trouble, hasn't he?"

"Heart? Not that I know of. Though he does look damned ill sometimes. But good God, man, he adores Anne. He wouldn't do anything to make her unhappy."

"Tell me everything you did when you came out of the dining room. No," Rick interrupted himself, "tell me what happened before dinner. I arrived very late, you know."

"As a matter of fact, I drove up at the same time as Deschamps. I parked behind him. He and his sister were having some sort of row, and then he saw me and said good evening and introduced me and so on and we walked into the building together."

"What were they rowing about?"

Steve shrugged. "My French isn't up to following a family spat between two Parisians. And I wasn't paying much attention anyway. When we got inside, the elevator was on its way up and we made stupid conversation while we waited. I asked about Mme. Trinquard's trip and so on. Then the elevator came and we went up. Anne and her uncle were already there. Let's see." Steve squinted in the effort to remember. "I think Arrietti was the next to arrive. Then Fresne. He ran me into a corner and tried to sell me some concrete."

"Is he in the concrete business?"

"Fresne has a finger in a lot of pies. Concrete's short here and he'd heard we needed some. Then Dorothy Vidal came in at the same time as Elting. Louise took her round and introduced her to Mme. Trinquard and said, 'You know Henri, don't you?' or something of the sort, and Deschamps said rather stiffly, 'I've met Mme. Vidal in the office.' Oh, I remember." Steve laughed at the recollection and then went on, "She said, 'Your brother is being very unkind to me,' and Mme. Trinquard said, 'He isn't usually, to blondes.' And the Vidal turned to Henri and said, 'It isn't even dyed,' and pulled up a curl. She was being all kitten-ish—about like a saber-toothed tiger. Then she went off to talk to someone and Elting talked to her, and when Fresne saw that he stopped trying to sell me concrete and went over and joined them."

"Are both of them interested in the widow Vidal?"

"In her or her cash. Elting is married, but his wife's away and I've heard she isn't coming back. The Cannings were the last to arrive before you. They looked as if they'd been rowing. They often do. But when they got there they be-haved fairly normally. There was the usual talk. About the wedding, about the fight, about this *Blithe Spirit* perform-ance. Nothing out of the ordinary."

"You didn't notice Deschamps particularly?"

"He was talking to Anne, mostly." A little while later he said, "Vanner, d'you have to go back to the States on the first plane you can get?"

"We'll have a look for the murderer first." Rick got up. "Now go home and go to bed. Your lying awake brooding won't help anyone."

After Sales had gone, Rick made a list of suspects. There

had been fourteen people at dinner. One was dead. He knew that he himself had not killed Deschamps. So that left him with twelve:

Steve Sales	Douglas and Gloria Canning
Louise and Bob Fareham	Fred Elting
Justine Trinquard	Dr. Arrietti
Anne Mantle	Dorothy Vidal
Howard Mantle	Michel Fresne

For the present, he didn't consider Sales, and he ruled out Anne and Justine as being unlikely. Being prejudiced in favor of his friends, he put Bob and Louise in the unlikely class as well. Bob seemed to have been in full sight most of the evening, mixing drinks, and he could think of no possible motive for Louise. She was fifty, she adored her husband, and therefore any kind of liaison with the much younger Deschamps was highly improbable. Louise had too good a sense of humor.

He still had seven. Gloria Canning, if she'd been conducting some kind of affair with Deschamps, might conceivably have killed him from jealousy. Likewise, if she'd been conducting an affair and her husband had found out, he might have decided on murder. They were possibles.

Howard Mantle had disapproved of Anne's marriage. As she had insisted on going ahead anyway, he might have decided to show his disapproval in drastic form. He was a possible.

Of the remaining four, Fred Elting appeared to be an objectionable person whose wife had gone away and people thought did not intend returning. Merely being objectionable, unfortunately, was no evidence that he had committed

59

murder. If there were some connection between the absent wife and Deschamps, perhaps, it might be possible.

Dorothy Vidal was a widow and attractive. Rick qualified his thought with "physically." Apparently her only relations with the dead man had been at the office. Which might or might not be so. But he rather wondered if the Frenchman could have put up with the self-dramatizing even for the sake of the long thighs and firm breasts which the black crepe dress had hinted at rather than revealed.

Alfredo Arrietti, the doctor, and Michel Fresne, the other Frenchman, seemed to have no possible motive. Fresne said he had never met Deschamps before. However, Rick knew so little about them that he put them in a bracket by themselves under the heading of "Not enough information to form a preliminary opinion." He looked at his list for some time. Five unlikelies. Three possibles. Two less probable possibles. Two "No opinion." And, he reflected ruefully, even the unlikelies had to be considered.

He drew another sheet of paper toward him and wrote down the schedule the *comisario* had finally arrived at. He headed it, inelegantly, "Trips to the can."

1. Louise and Gloria. Saw nobody.
2. Elting.   Ditto.
3. Louise returns.   Ditto.
4. Elting returns.   Ditto.
5. Fresne goes.   Ditto.
6. Dorothy Vidal goes Ditto.
7. Canning goes. Finds door locked.
8. Gloria returns. Saw nobody.
9. Canning returns.   Ditto.
10. Fresne returns. Saw nobody.
11. Mantle goes to study. Ditto.

12. Dorothy Vidal returns. Saw Mantle.
13. Anne goes. Sees Vidal in arch of living room.
14. Anne returns. Sees nobody.
15. Sales goes. Sees nobody until he finds body.
16. Canning goes. Sees nobody till he finds Sales and body.

It was, Rick supposed, possible for them to have gone back and forth without seeing, or at least without noticing, other people. But it was remarkable split-second timing. He considered it for a long time and started to get undressed. As he did so he returned at intervals to the desk and looked at it, and finally picked it up and took it to bed with him. It was six o'clock when he put out the light.

CHAPTER 5

The insistent ringing of the telephone bell woke Rick. He looked at his watch as he reached out his hand for the instrument and saw that it was half-past seven. His voice was not agreeable as he said, "*Aquí habla Richard Vanner.*" As he listened, a puzzled frown drew his brows together. The speaker was the United States consul.

"Arrested?" Rick said when the consul stopped. "If they were going to do it, why wasn't it done last night?"

"He only spoke to me for a minute. Evidently he had insisted on his right to call his consul. And he knows my home number. He asked me to get you."

"Where is he?"

"At the Central. Calle Moreno."

"Okay. I'll get along there."

"Get in touch with me as soon as you have any information."

Rick grunted, hung up, and swung his legs over the side of the bed. He lighted a cigarette and then reached for the phone again and dialed a Defensa number. It was the home number of Jorge Seminario, a detective who handled Argentine inquiries for him when he didn't want to come down in person.

Seminario also did not sound too pleased to be called at seven-thirty. However, the North American, Señor Vanner, was a good customer who always paid promptly for the replies to his cabled or telephoned inquiries, and this time, while the Señor Vanner had been here himself, he had made no complaint about the amount of the bill rendered for the services of various operatives.

"Murder!" he exclaimed when Rick inquired whom he knew who would be useful. "Ah, you want to buy him free."

"I want to prove him innocent," corrected Rick.

"That may be more difficult," said Seminario. There was a pause during which Rick could imagine him rubbing the bald spot on the top of his head while his eyes rested on the gold chain that adorned his generous stomach. Jorge Seminario was rubbing the bald spot but he was looking at his third pajama button.

"I want to know what the police are doing. Sit in while they question witnesses. That sort of thing."

"Then it is my good friend, Señor Boggia, that you must go to. He is the brother of my brother-in-law. He is the *subjefe de la Sección de Investigaciones*." As he listened to Seminario adding instructions, Rick wondered if the detective were related to every official in the entire government. Never mind what the problem, he always knew someone on the inside who could help solve it.

"I also need information about the following." Rick read

out his list of names. "And put a tail on Fresne, Vidal, Mantle, and Canning."

Very little more than half an hour later Rick was shown into *subjefe* Boggia's office. He explained himself and showed papers. Señor Boggia listened quietly, his dark oblique eyes expressionless. He did not fit his name, which to Rick's mind suggested something rotund. Boggia was spare to the point of thinness.

Señor Boggia didn't much like North Americans, but there was something about this tall, gray-eyed man that impressed him. Annapolis and the navy had put a certain stamp on the clean-cut features, and years of intelligence work had drawn lines round the hard mouth. It was a disciplined face. He didn't look, thought Boggia, anywhere near the fifty years with which his passport credited him. After a while Boggia said, "The Señor Comandante seems to be suffering from a misapprehension."

"Probably a great many, señor," Rick told him cheerfully. "To which particular one do you refer?"

"Sales has not been arrested. He was brought in for questioning."

"There isn't much difference, is there?"

"A technical one. Further . . ." Boggia paused.

"Yes?"

"It was not in connection with the death of Henri Deschamps."

"In connection with what?"

"The murder of Fred Elting."

Rick's face was expressionless. He leaned back in his chair and took cigarettes from his pocket. He offered one to Boggia and asked, "When was Elting killed?"

"Sometime early this morning. I have not yet seen the medical report."

"How was it done?"

"He was shot in the entrance of his apartment house." The *subjefe* leaned forward and offered a lighter. "It was reported that Sales had had a quarrel with him last night and attempted to kill him. Sales could not account for his movements during the early hours of this morning."

"He was with me until pretty late," said Rick.

"*Sí*, señor, but after that he said he drove and he does not seem to know where. Does it seem probáble to you, señor, that at that hour of the night, or rather morning, when he left you, a man would just go for a drive without a definite object?"

"I have done things like that myself. If I thought I could not get to sleep. May I see Sales?"

Steve looked as if he hadn't slept but he greeted Rick quite cheerfully. "Won't even let their prisoners shave before they drag 'em in. One looks the part more, I suppose." A little later he said, in answer to a question of Rick's, "I can't make them understand that I wasn't going to kill Elting last night when you hauled me off. They don't realize the difference between slapping a man down because he is out of order and shooting him from ambush."

"Where did you go when you left me?"

"I just drove. That's the hell of it. Out past the airport."

"Whyinhell didn't you go home to bed?" growled Rick.

"How was I to know I'd need an alibi? Anyway, I wouldn't have had one if I had gone home. Remind me to pick up a blonde tonight so I'll have one."

65

Another police official came out and informed Sales that he might go and thanked him for his co-operation.

"Co-operation, hell!" snorted Steve. "They sent a squad to get me."

Señor Boggia came back. He was, he told Rick, looking forward to co-operating with the distinguished American.

"I'd like to be shown where Elting was found," said Rick.

The *subjefe* gave practical and prompt proof of his desire to co-operate. He called a sad-looking subordinate, who nodded his head eagerly when he received instructions, in the manner of a mandarin doll. He was told to take a police car and conduct the distinguished North American señor to see anything he wanted to.

"Go home and try to have alibis in case anyone else gets killed," Rick told Steve.

"D'you think the two are connected?"

"Don't you?"

The apartment house where Fred Elting had lived was in Calle Esmeralda, in the center of the town. On the street level was a tailor, and the three next floors were occupied by business offices. A heavy glass door led from the street into a large imitation-marble hall. Fifteen feet farther along was another pair of glass doors, not quite so heavy as the first. Beyond them was a continuation of the marble hall. On the left were two elevators, facing each other with about four feet between. Farther back, in the right-hand corner, was a small circular desk behind which, during the daytime, the porter sat.

"He had fallen here." The sad little official pointed to a spot on the ground in front of the farther elevator. "His body made it difficult to open the door. The maid from the fifth floor rang the signal for the elevator, rode down in it, and when she tried to open the door here, she couldn't. So after a while she rode back up to the third floor and got into the other elevator. When she got down she saw it."

"That was at a quarter to six?"

The official nodded frantically. "She was going to Mass, but she became hysterical instead."

"And he was shot in the back?"

More nodding. "The *señor subjefe* thinks the murderer might have concealed himself behind the porter's desk."

"I wonder how many tenants arrived home between four and six this morning."

"It is being inquired into."

Rick went back and looked at the numbered bells out on the street, outside the first glass doors. "What's the system? You ring the bell and the party opens the door from upstairs?"

"Oh no, señor." The idea seemed to horrify the official. "You speak to the party on that phone and then they come down and open for you."

Rick was silent. No chance that the murderer had just rung all the bells in the hope that someone in some apartment would press a buzzer and release the lock.

"So it remains," continued the official, "that the only possible way that the murderer could have got in was to have waited until some tenant went in or out."

"Unless the murderer lived in the building," suggested Rick. He wandered over to the light switch. It was of the type that when lighted remained on for two or three minutes, supposedly long enough for a person to have found his

67

way to the elevator and pressed the signal. "And of course nobody will have heard the shot," he grumbled to himself, then turned back to the official. "Have they got the bullet yet?"

"The autopsy is at eleven."

Rick thanked the official profusely for his courtesy and, as he was within a few blocks of the United States Consulate in the Boston Bank Building, he walked down there.

The consul wasn't happy and he reported that the ambassador was worried. "Old man Sales is not only indecently rich, but a fighter," he said, "and the moment he gets to hear of this he'll stir things up."

"Sales isn't arrested yet," Rick pointed out.

"What d'you think of it?" asked the consul. "Off the record. Did he do it?"

Rick was looking at a blank spot on the wall above a calendar. After a while he said, "In murder cases, I always try to keep an open mind. The most improbable people sometimes commit murder. However, I had Sales under me for a short time in the Aleutians and I don't find it easy to believe that he stabbed one man in the back and shot another from behind."

"Apart from our personal opinion of Steve, things look pretty bad for him."

"The only thing is that nobody has supplied a plausible reason for his killing Deschamps in such a manner. If you take the motive as jealousy, which is the only motive that's come to light so far, why should he do it in that way and at that time? He must have been jealous ever since the engagement was announced, and he must have had thousands of better opportunities to kill Deschamps if he wanted to."

"Unless he figured that in the confusion of a dinner party he could get away with it."

"And remembered that the Farehams had a suitable weapon on display? Suppose they'd lost the dagger? Put it away? The maid was cleaning it?" Rick shook his head. "Men bent on murder don't leave the weapon to chance."

"If it wasn't premeditated——" The consul stopped.

"Then something happened at the Farehams' house so that someone had an urgent need to kill Deschamps and do it quickly. And why on earth should Steve need to kill him quickly?"

"Possibly seeing him with Anne just drove the jealousy over the edge. Don't think I believe Steve did it. I don't. I'm just pointing out the arguments against him."

"I know them," said Rick a bit grimly. He got up. "I'd better go and dig up some arguments for him. Oh, and the reason I came here. I want to talk to someone in the French Embassy. Who's there? Anyone I know? Failing that, give me a note to someone."

In the end he left with a note from the American ambassador to the French one, who received him courteously and seemed disposed to do anything he could to help the investigation.

"I don't want to ask questions that are out of order," Rick said, "but can you tell me if you know of anything connected with Deschamps' work for you that could possibly have put him in any danger?"

The ambassador shook his head quite definitely. "There was absolutely nothing."

"And anything from his work in Rio de Janeiro, before he came here?"

"As far as I know, nothing. I have already queried my colleague in Rio."

"I want to canvass all possibilities," said Rick.

"You do not believe that this countryman of yours killed him?"

Rick outlined his reasons for not believing it. "None of them are concrete," he admitted, "and they are worthless in court."

"Mme. Trinquard, his sister, is inclined to agree with you. She called me last night about some confidential papers that he had at the apartment, as it appears that the police wanted to go over them."

"I want to see her, if she feels up to it."

"Mme. Trinquard is a remarkable woman. Her record in the resistance and her career with her newspaper both show it. I think you will find her eager to help you if you sincerely wish to find her brother's murderer and not just to clear your compatriot."

"I think the only way to clear Sales completely is to find the murderer. Otherwise there'll always be a doubt in people's minds."

"I don't think Henri was a happy man," said the ambassador a little later. "Not that he ever said anything. It is just an impression. But there are so many like that, since the war."

"I believe Dorothy Vidal has been here to see Deschamps about something?" The ambassador nodded, and Rick continued, "I'd like permission to see what you have in your files about the matter."

There was silence. Vanner could feel the ambassador's bright, wise eyes considering him. After a while he said, "Very well. But it must be confidential."

"Of course."

The ambassador appeared satisfied, picked up the phone, and gave some orders. A confidential clerk appeared very bewildered by the instructions he received. He kept looking at Rick and murmuring, "Not a Frenchman. Not even police," as he led him to another office and started to open a safe, ostentatiously putting his body between the detective and the safe as if he suspected Rick of a desire to learn the combination.

"This is the file dealing with Mme. Vidal's petition," the clerk announced finally, laying a folder in front of Rick.

"Simply applying for permission to take her capital out of France," said Rick, after looking through the papers. "The capital left by her late husband."

"Yes. Mme. Vidal was not herself of French nationality before her marriage with M. Vidal."

"Yes. And . . . ?"

"It complicates the transfer of funds."

"Quite. And this process about the late Jacques Vidal's property?"

"Ah, monsieur, that is something else." The clerk laid an unwilling hand on some of the other papers he had taken from the safe. "You understand that people who were convicted of collaborating with the enemy had their property confiscated?"

"Yes."

"Sometimes they were convicted *in absentia*."

"And . . . ?"

71

"In those cases, property in France or in French territory was confiscated."

"And had the late Jacques Vidal been convicted?"

"No."

"What bearing had it on the matter?"

"None."

Rick lighted a cigarette and kept his temper. He said, "Then why is this process included in the file?"

"Investigations were proceeding to establish whether, while in this country, he had collaborated with the enemy."

"I see. And where are the results of these investigations?"

"In this file."

Rick held out his hand for it and settled back in the chair and started to read the closely typewritten pages. It was a detailed account of the relations of the Vichy representative with the German Embassy in Buenos Aires before the Argentine had declared war. It established, without apparent doubt, that Vidal had, prior to 1939, been an intimate friend of the first secretary, a man named Jean Fremont, who had remained in the service of the Vichy regime. There seemed no evidence that the friendship had continued after 1941.

Then something else caught Rick's eyes. "It was widely rumored that Mme. Vidal was, at that time, conducting an affair with Jean Fremont."

There were more details of quasi-diplomatic exchanges between the Vichy representative and the German ambassador. Jean Fremont had, it appeared, been active socially, and later had been accused of being the Buenos Aires head of one section of the espionage ring which had been organized in South America.

When Argentine had finally declared war against Germany, Fremont had disappeared, and two months later turned up in France. In one of the earliest of the collaborationist trials after the liberation, he had been condemned and shot.

There had been various rumors that Jacques Vidal was involved with the Nazi spy ring. At the time of Fremont's trial some papers taken from Fremont had listed a Vidal among the people from whom he had received information. Also, among papers taken from a known Nazi agent apprehended in Montevideo, there was a mention of Vidal.

A number of Vidal's friends and acquaintances had dropped him as a result of these rumors, and in March of 1945 he had died of ptomaine poisoning following a buffet supper at the house of Alfred Turgensen. Nobody else had been ill as a result of the food, and there had been more rumors, though no proof, of foul play.

The next batch of papers was a petition made in 1946 by Dorothy Vidal for the establishment of her dower right in Vidal's estate in France. This had required endless papers to back up the claim and there was a thick file of correspondence. There were letters from notaries, letters referring to photostats of records. It was all quite routine, but it had taken until the end of 1947 to get together all the papers necessary, signed and sealed by the proper authorities.

At that time the Paris end reported that decision on the matter was withheld pending some inquiries being made into the alleged collaborationist activities of the late Jacques Vidal. After the passage of five months the correspondence started again with the information that the process was being transferred back to Buenos Aires for further investigation.

73

Rick smiled grimly. It was all so typical of the red tape of any government. At that point it had been handed to Deschamps to investigate.

"Why not to a consular officer?" asked Rick.

"M. l'Ambassadeur wished M. Deschamps to be responsible for it," said the clerk.

Deschamps had made a number of notes. From them, Rick concluded that he had made a careful study of the files in connection with the Fremont case, as paragraphs in the files were frequently referred to.

"Will you ask M. Deschamps' secretary to come in?"

The clerk looked at the file, at the safe, and at Rick.

"Either phone for him or shut it," suggested Vanner.

"If M. l'Ambassadeur said——"

"That make you happier?" Rick reached out his foot and kicked the safe door shut.

"Monsieur understands——"

"Perfectly."

Looking a bit relieved, the clerk disappeared and returned in a minute with a young man who said his name was de Large. Vanner explained his mission. "There are several names and addresses jotted down here. They looked as if they might have something to do with the investigations about Vidal."

De Large looked at the papers for a while. "M. Deschamps was very interested in this affair," he said at last. "He told me that he thought half the truth had not yet come out." He stopped and frowned at the sheet of paper. Rick didn't try to hurry him. At last he said, "I wonder. Yes, it might be. One time M. Deschamps was trying to get the addresses of the two maids who worked for Vidal during 1944 and 1945. These names and addresses—look! One of them is in the Boca and there are no telephone numbers. They could be maids."

"He was making a detailed investigation," murmured Rick.

"He was bitter about collaborationists," said de Large. "Even more so about those who were over here and quite safe and just did it for money. He could see some excuse for someone who was in France, with a gun to their head, as it were. I remember his saying one time, 'A man who had a family and knew they'd lose their food cards or be shot or put in a camp if he were caught helping the resistance, well, there's a lot of excuse for him. But for these *salauds* here——'"

Rick nodded. He was copying down the addresses.

"I asked him about a week ago if there was anything new on the Vidal matter," went on de Large. "Mme. Vidal had asked me if I could find out what was happening."

"You know her?"

"I have met her at parties and so on. She seemed in considerable distress about the whole matter. And it is sometimes very hard on families who cannot get any of their money owing to something like this that is not their fault, though I understand Mme. Vidal got all of his Argentine estate, which was considerable."

"She appears to be quite prosperous," said Rick.

"She certainly dresses very well," agreed de Large. "She has a—a *je ne sais quoi*——"

"Sex appeal," said Rick dryly. "Long thighs, neat ankles, and nice breasts."

"She certainly has that. One wonders——"

75

"Why don't you try?"

"I can't afford a *poule de luxe,* monsieur. Life here—the prices—in the last year they have doubled, and our living allowance never keeps pace with them." He paused a moment and then said, "There is something else about Mme. Vidal. A certain *tristesse*—perhaps."

Rick thought of her conversation at dinner but he didn't say anything. De Large was very young. "Did she come in frequently?"

"Not often. But a few weeks ago M. Deschamps wrote and asked her to come."

"What was the interview about?"

"I was not present, but I believe he wanted to ask her some questions about the Fremont affair. It was after she had gone that day that he said he thought not more than half the truth had come out. There is one other thing," went on de Large, a bit diffidently. "About three weeks ago M. Deschamps said he was being followed. But he never did anything about it that I know of and he never mentioned it again."

"He didn't say who he thought might be responsible?"

"No. Just that the man was clever and he hadn't been able to get a good look at him."

CHAPTER 6

It was still too early to expect a result from the Elting autopsy, so Vanner took a cab and directed the driver to Calle Sargento Cabral. As his cab rounded the corner of the road he saw Gloria Canning coming out of a building and start walking toward a parked car. He said *"Pare"* and thrust a five-peso note into the hand of his startled but delighted driver and got out. He managed to reach Gloria as a chauffeur came round to open the door for her.

She greeted him effusively and ran on, "—and I'm hardly ever in town before lunch but my mother's staying with us and she takes so much time and there's the play tonight. It'll be a ghastly performance but these things do raise money painlessly. I've millions of things to get. I always have to be in their plays because I was in the theater once. It's so nice you haven't gone. Someone said last night that you were leaving today. This is a dreadful town for that. You meet people and just get to know them and then they go."

"Or get murdered," said Rick.

"Don't talk about it. It's all too ghastly. And I'd always thought Steve Sales so nice."

"You seem very sure he did it."

"Well, I mean, there he was with the dagger in his hand. And this isn't a film where the murderer turns out to be someone who had a cast-iron alibi in Patagonia or Brazil or something. I mean, in real life it's usually the obvious person who did it, isn't it?"

"Sometimes. Not always."

"You're not——" She stopped. "Are you working on it?" He nodded. "Oh. I hadn't thought of that."

"If you know anything useful, you might give me a spot of help. I could use it." Rick had a charming smile when he wanted to use it.

But it didn't do him any good. She rattled some more about the "millions" of things she had to do, and finally he closed the car door and watched her drive off. He walked along the block until he reached the number of Deschamps' apartment building. It was the door Gloria had come out from. If she had called on Justine Trinquard, wouldn't it have been more natural to have mentioned it?

The maid, Dolores, was flustered and she looked as if she had been crying. She ushered Rick straight into the living room without any attempt to consult Justine, who was telephoning, as to whether she wished to receive the visitor.

Justine turned, the phone still held to her ear, and a fleeting irritation crossed her tired face. It was quickly banished by a conventional expression. She put her hand over the transmitter and said, "Excuse me. Please sit down."

She spoke rapid French, evidently to someone in the embassy. "—and you can reach me there. It will be better for your people to make a statement for all the papers. Thanks. Yes, thanks. You're very kind."

She put down the phone and turned to Vanner. Briefly he explained his visit and saw the veiled irritation disappear.

"I knew so little of Henri's life here," she said, and passed her hand momentarily across her eyes.

"And you're dead tired," said Rick. "I hate having to bother you."

"The police were here most of the night, going through his papers," she explained. "He had brought some work home and I had to reach the ambassador." She was silent for a moment and then went on. "I want to see my brother's murderer caught, Mr. Vanner. But I also want to be quite sure it is the right man." Again she stopped and he didn't speak. "After the liberation, I saw——" She seemed to be fishing for a word.

"Miscarriages of justice," suggested Rick.

"Yes. You understand. There were many. Some honest mistakes because passions ran high and men who have been schooled in violence and killing for six years do not always wait to sift evidence. Then there were others. People who cashed in on a wave of feeling to prosecute their private feuds. This young American—Sales—Henri had spoken of him." A tired little smile touched her lips for a second. "He told me that Sales was in love with Anne and said, 'He is a much better man than I am, but I'm glad she isn't smart enough to know it.' I know Henri liked him and respected him, and Henri usually did not like Americans. Forgive me, monsieur."

"We aren't popular as a nation," agreed Rick with a smile. "You don't feel that Sales is guilty?"

79

"It is an argument of no consequence. But Henri was shrewd about people. I do not think he would have liked and respected a man who would stab in the back."

"I know Sales a bit," Rick told her, "and my argument is the same. I've handled a good many men in my day, and one gets to be able to judge them. If Sales didn't do it, then who did?" She didn't reply and he went on. "What did the police find among his papers?"

"Nothing of interest to them. They finally made notes of two or three telephone numbers scribbled down on a pad by the telephone. There were no names." She got up and went into the little hall and returned with the pad. "Oh— excuse me. Will you have something to drink?"

Rick looked at her tired face and said, "Sit down and I'll get you something."

"A brandy, please."

When he'd given her the drink and made himself a whisky and soda he said, "What was Gloria Canning doing here?"

"She said she came to offer help," replied Justine.

"And she did come?"

Again the tired little smile crossed her face. "I am not quite sure."

"Tell me what you think."

"I am saying something which is only an opinion. I think she had written some notes or letters to Henri at some time and wanted to see if she could find them. She tried to look at the desk, but I did not give her the chance. I learned about those things during the occupation," she explained. "Then I told her that the police had already been through Henri's papers. She seemed upset, so I assured her that he never kept letters. She was obviously relieved and she left."

"Hm. Had your brother spoken about her?"

Justine was silent. She was weighing in her mind whether to tell this quiet, competent American everything she knew and suspected. Her brain was too tired to think very coherently. All she was conscious of was weariness, physical, mental, and spiritual. The night before, as she had knelt beside her brother's body, the one thought in her mind had been gratitude that her father was dead. The frail old man, whose only interest in life since the death of his wife had been his children, could not have borne the loss of his other son. Now, she just felt tired. It didn't matter very much. There was only herself to feel the loss and she wouldn't live forever. To Anne she gave a fleeting sympathy. But Anne was young and hadn't seen everything crumble bit by bit around her. Anne would forget.

Rick sat patiently, smoking, drinking his drink, and saying nothing. At last she spoke, rapidly. "Henri was the youngest. My elder brother was very serious. Very ambitious. He was a doctor. Before the war, Henri played the fool. Women ran after him and he enjoyed it. He always had some *grande affaire* going, not usually for long. He enjoyed life. He was reckless, thoughtless. He was stationed in Saigon and Tonkin. He was always off on some mad escapade. Then he met Geneviève de Faure. Her parents were stationed in Haiphong and she had to be sent home because her health couldn't stand the climate.

"Henri worshiped her. It was a surprise to us and to his friends. Geneviève was a saint. I don't mean she was dreary or smug. She wasn't. She was gay and ready for anything.

81

The marriage was arranged. For the first time in his life, Henri loved. He wasn't just 'in love.'

"Then the war came. He was called up with his class. He was wounded and taken prisoner. We didn't know whether he was alive or dead. When it was inevitable that Paris would be occupied, we tried to persuade Geneviève to go. But she wouldn't. The aunt with whom she was living packed up and got to Cannes and subsequently to Brazil. It was a hard winter, that first winter of the occupation."

She stopped for a moment, then went on again. "My older brother was shot, summarily, for operating on a man who had been wounded escaping from the police. Our food cards were taken from us. Geneviève too, because she had come to live with us. We did what we could. But her lungs —she needed good food, warmth. She got wet one day. There was no coal. Pneumonia followed, and in three days she was dead.

"A couple of months later, Henri escaped. He made his way to Paris. I hardly recognized him, the condition he was in. One thing had been keeping him alive. The thought of Geneviève." Justine gave a little shrug.

"When he was fit to travel, he got to England. They used him as liaison between the headquarters in England and us. They always said he had a charmed life. He drank too much, he worked too hard—and any woman who came along——" Again she stopped. "But always the women were very earthy, very demimondaine, as different from Geneviève as possible. That went on until the end of 1943. December twenty-fourth we were both picked up by the Gestapo in St. Malo. While we were in prison our father died.

"After the liberation, when he was appointed to Brazil, Henri said to me, 'A country that doesn't know what a war is all about, where you can fill your belly every day and take a woman to bed every night without wondering if she's in the pay of the Gestapo! That is heaven!'" She got up and refilled Rick's glass, saying half apologetically, "I've told you all that because I wanted you to understand what it had done to him."

Rick nodded. The pattern was not an uncommon one and he had seen it before. He found himself wondering what it had done to the woman in front of him who spoke so wearily and dispassionately of it all. He walked over to the piano and picked up the photo of Anne Mantle. "Anne is quite unlike Geneviève?"

"Absolutely."

"And so is Gloria Canning?" She nodded and he went on, "You were going to tell me something about Gloria."

Briefly she recounted having seen Gloria and Henri on Cangallo the day before. "Anne did not see him. I, of course, said nothing."

"You say Anne recognized the house?"

"Evidently her uncle had pointed it out to her, and the chauffeur was reticent about it. He just said he believed it to be an *amueblado*."

"That's what they call them here."

"I liked Anne. So, with the privilege of an older sister, I asked about Gloria. He said, 'God preserve me from passionate women.' I made some remark about his never having shown any desire to be preserved from them, and he said, 'One can't get rid of them,' and went on to say he thought

83

the best thing to do was to let it taper off and die a natural death.

"It seemed to me dangerous, because though Anne in theory is broad-minded and thinks she understands everything, I was afraid she'd be badly hurt if she found out."

"When did you have this discussion with your brother?"

"En route over to the dinner at the Farehams'."

"And it was quite an argument?"

"Yes. He got annoyed because I thought Canning suspected." She recounted the brief conversation between Deschamps and Canning at Mantle's house two nights before. "And when I met Gloria at the Farehams', I knew that it was her voice that had telephoned just after I arrived and hung up very suddenly when she discovered who I was."

It opened up various possibilities. Rick pulled cigarettes from his pocket and held them out to her. "One other line has occurred to me. Was there anybody at the dinner whom you'd met before you came to Buenos Aires or whom Henri had known before?"

"Henri had known Bob Fareham rather briefly in Paris just before the war. He met him through some friends when he'd just arrived back from Saigon. I'd never met them."

"Of the guests, there was no one?"

She shook her head. "Canning I had met at Mantle's house. None of the others. The doctor, Arrietti. Mrs. Vidal. The man who sat on my right—a Frenchman. Fresne, was that his name? Nor Sales. Nor the other American."

"Elting?"

"I didn't hear his name."

"He was murdered this morning."

If Rick had expected Justine to show any reaction, he was disappointed. After a second's pause she said, "He seemed an unpleasant young man, but why was he murdered?"

"We don't know—yet. But the obvious reason would be because he knew something about the killing of your brother." After a little while he asked, "Mantle opposed Anne's marriage to Henri. Did he talk to you about it?"

"He was perfectly frank. He said he thought Anne was mistaking the glamour of worldliness and the background of war, the Far East and so on, for love and that Henri was too old for her. He also thought, though he was too polite to say so to me in so many words, that he was after her money."

"Was he?"

"From Henri's point of view, it was a very suitable marriage," said Justine. "At the same time, he was genuinely fond of Anne."

"I see."

The front doorbell rang and Dolores bustled out, looking harassed. Again without any preliminary inquiry, she ushered Michel Fresne into the room. He seemed a trifle disconcerted to see Rick and tugged at his upper lip.

"I felt perhaps, madame, I could render some small services," he said formally. "I know the town fairly well."

"You are very kind, but the Embassy is taking care of everything for me. Won't you sit down?"

"Ah yes. The Embassy." He glanced at Vanner. "Somebody told me last night, monsieur, that you are a detective."

Rick nodded. "Steve Sales asked me to take a hand in

this. Mme. Trinquard has been kind enough to clear up some points for me."

"You do not feel that M. Sales is guilty?"

"Do you?" asked Rick bluntly.

Fresne shrugged. "I would not have thought it, but he is found with the knife and——" Another shrug finished the sentence.

"Yes. Looked bad," agreed Rick. "By the way, I think I heard you say last night that you'd never met Madame's brother before?"

"I had never had the pleasure."

"Seems odd, in a place like this. There's only a small French colony."

"Monsieur, I do not cultivate the society of the foreign— I should say—the French colony. My observation is that if one arrives in a foreign country and associates with the Embassy crowd, one never learns anything about the country and seldom makes useful business contacts. I am a businessman. I want to do business with the Argentines. For that, I must know them. If I go always and listen to my fellow countrymen bemoaning that they are not at home in France . . . I am sure Madame knows how the French live when they are abroad."

"I agree," said Justine. "They form a tight little colony and never see anyone outside it. And they do sit around and suffer from nostalgia."

"The Americans and English do much the same," laughed Rick. "How long have you been here, M. Fresne?"

"Since 1945."

"Nineteen forty-five." Justine repeated it; she was looking at Fresne with a faintly puzzled expression.

Rick said, "I suppose the police have been round to ask you when you last saw Elting?"

Fresne made a face. "At a quarter to eight this morning, they came. And I could tell them nothing. We left Mme. Vidal's together. He had his car and I had mine. That is the last I saw of him."

"What time was this?"

"It was a quarter past four when we left her apartment. I remember saying she should get to bed. She is a highly nervous woman—very sensitive—and the events of the evening had been a strain on everyone."

"Where did you go when you left her?"

"To my apartment, and the police seem to think that I should be able to produce someone who saw me come in. But at half-past four we have no porter on duty and, unfortunately, I do not even have a servant who sleeps on the premises. One does not expect to need two alibis in one night."

Rick got up. "I rather doubt whether anyone will have much of an alibi for that hour in the morning," he said carelessly, and turned to Justine. "Thank you for your help, madame."

"If you want to reach me, I'll be at the Mantles'. Anne called again about my staying there until after the funeral, so——" She gave a little shrug. "She's sending the car in for me this afternoon."

"I'm at the Plaza, if I can be of any use to you," said Rick.

"If there is nothing in which I can be of service," said Fresne, "I will not intrude."

"Really, there is nothing, thanks. It was kind of you to

87

come." She came with them to the door. "Let me know, Mr. Vanner, if you find out anything."

In the elevator Fresne inquired if he could give Rick a lift. "Yes, thanks. To the Morgue."

"Mon Dieu! Are you serious?" The dapper little man moved into the far corner of the elevator.

"Where they take the corpses."

"But of course! I will be very happy." Fresne did not sound it. "But where is it? Believe me, I know the town fairly well, but I have never before had occasion to go to the Morgue."

"Faculty of Medicine," Rick told him.

When the intricacies of getting out of the parking place had been dealt with, the Frenchman said, "Do you not feel that Mme. Trinquard should have a bodyguard?"

"Why?"

"It is the police theory that Elting was killed because he knew something about the murder of Deschamps; does it not follow that she is in danger?"

"Only if she knows something."

"But if the murderer thinks she does?"

"Why should he?"

A taxi that had been parked on Sargento Cabral was still behind them. Fresne was watching it in the driving mirror. Rick saw the muscles round his mouth tauten and he shot recklessly in front of a *colectivo*.

"You're nervous," remarked the detective.

"Frankly, yes, monsieur. I was with Elting last night, and if this murderer does not mind how many people he kills, he may imagine that Elting told me whatever it was he knew. I must admit that I do not like the idea."

"Did Elting tell you anything?"

"All the morning I have asked myself that. I can think of nothing. We talked of the murder, of course. But he had nothing to say which had not been said at the Farehams'. M. Vanner"—he turned earnestly and for a moment disregarded his driving and earned an angry toot from the horn of a car he endangered—"I am very relieved that you are investigating. I should like to help you, if I may. I have had some small experience of police work. Perhaps I could be of service to you."

Why was there always somebody in every case who felt the urge to be a detective? thought Rick. "If there is anything you can do, I'll let you know," he replied with intentional vagueness.

"Frankly, monsieur, my motives are selfish. The sooner this is cleared up, the sooner I shall not have to wonder if I should buy a bulletproof vest." He gave a short laugh. "You think me a coward, monsieur, and probably you are right. Ten years ago, I might not have minded. But now——" There was something attractive about his confession. He did not try to excuse or explain. Perhaps he knew that those things cannot be explained to someone who does not understand, and those who do understand need no explanation.

"Did you know Elting well?" asked Rick a half block farther on.

"Not well. I had met him originally at some cocktail party, I think. Then I had done a few business deals with him."

"What kind of business?"

"Machine tools. He had an outlet for certain kinds, and the American firms supplying him couldn't ship for six months. I had some in Uruguay which he sold through his outlets. I handle any kind of business at all, monsieur. I will buy or sell real estate or ladies' stockings, insurance or exchange. In these days one never knows where a profit may be."

"Exchange is pretty profitable right now," remarked Rick idly.

"Doubtless for you, who have dollars to sell in the black market," said Fresne dryly. "But for the importer and exporter!" He broke off suddenly and said, "That is the same taxi! You have not noticed?"

"Long before you nearly drove us into a *colectivo* to get away from it," Rick told him. "This is the Morgue here, I think. Down the side. Where are you going when you leave me?"

Fresne was staring intently in the driving mirror and bumped the curb as he drew in. He wet dry lips and said, "To my office."

"I'll take care of the taxi. Wait until you see me go up to him and then drive off."

"But what can you do?"

"I'm used to these things. Good-by and thanks for the lift."

The taxi had stopped at the other side of the road, some thirty yards back. Rick crossed to it and opened the door, paying no attention to the indignant "This is occupied" of the man inside.

"You work for Jorge Seminario," he said. "I'm the client. Don't follow Fresne at present. He's going back to his office. Pick him up again there and try not to be seen next time." As he spoke, Rick saw the Frenchman drive off. As soon as his car turned the corner, Rick crossed back to the imposing building which houses the Morgue and walked up the steps, admiring the graceful marble nude on her marble couch which faced him as he entered.

It took him a few minutes to explain what he wanted at the reception office, then a man conducted him downstairs through a series of corridors adorned with statues and bas-relief. The autopsy room was functional, when they reached it. At one of the tables two doctors were working and they both seemed annoyed.

"Since eleven o'clock!" one of them exclaimed when the attendant told him Rick's errand. "This bullet must have gone in circles."

While Rick was debating whether to wait or not, the *comisario* who had questioned them at the Fareham house came in. "The *subjefe* of the *Sección de Investigaciones* explained that the señor was interesting himself in the case," he said politely.

Rick inquired how they were progressing on the Elting end of the case. The *comisario* explained that he was working in close co-operation with the *comisario* of the district where Elting had been murdered. "First, it was necessary to find out where everyone who had been at the dinner was. So far, it has been unsatisfactory. As you know, Señor Sales was driving round. Dr. Arrietti went home with Señor Mantle and his niece, then went to his own home. He lives alone and his servant did not hear him come in. Mme. Vidal was accompanied home by the Señores Elting and Fresne. Her maid did not hear them come in or leave. Señor Fresne lives alone. Señor Canning and his señora went home. You, señor, went with Señor Sales, and it is reported that you did not leave your room until this morning at seven fifty-five."

"Right," grinned Rick, "though I might have crept out by the service elevator. It's automatic."

"You see! There is no proof of anything!" The *comisario* was dramatic. "It may interest the señor to know," he went on, "that the contents of the glass found on the bathroom floor had been only soda water."

Before Rick had time to comment, an exclamation of triumph came from one of the doctors. He had the bullet. "*Gracias á Dios!* I have a luncheon engagement and I thought I was never going to find it. It entered here——" Elting dressed in his somewhat loud suit had not been too prepossessing a specimen, but Elting on the marble autopsy table was somehow repulsive. The doctor went on being technical. Rick nodded absent-mindedly. He was not very interested in the freak course of the bullet through the Elting cadaver. The bullet interested him. He looked at it through the lens someone passed him. Nine mm. or .38 short. He handed it back to the *comisario*, who regarded its flattened condition sadly.

"My bet is that it's a Belgian Browning," said Rick, "but I'm afraid even your ballistics department won't be sure."

"And there are so many foreign guns in the town, señor," said the *comisario*, "and so few registered."

Rick saw a phone and asked permission to use it. He called Steve Sales at his office. "What kind of gun have you?"

"Colt automatic. Forty-four."

"Thank God for that," said Rick. "Have lunch with me?"

"Sure. Where are you?"

"At the Morgue. No, they don't serve lunch here. Or maybe they do. I didn't ask." From the tail of his eye he could see into a small room which contained an electric stove, probably to make coffee for the personnel. "I think the Plaza would be better."

When Rick turned to say good-by to the doctors, the *comisario* said, "The Señor Sales?"

"Yes. His gun's a .44."

"Many people have more than one gun."

"I've a friend with over a hundred," agreed Rick. "He collects them. *Hasta luego.*"

CHAPTER 7

Sales was in the bar on his second whisky when Rick arrived. "Two distinguished members of our American colony were so busy trying not to see me," he said, "that they walked straight into a table. They looked rather funny. I've been tried by the *Herald* and the *Standard* and found guilty."

"How about *Prensa* and *La Nación?* I haven't had time to see the papers."

"They don't count from the point of view of the American-Anglo-Argentine colony. They never read 'em. They have reserved judgment, by the way. They always do."

"Jury not in agreement? That's all to the good." Rick gave him an edited version of his morning's activities.

"This story is going to be in the evening papers tonight in New York," said Steve.

"And——"

"You don't know my father, do you?"

"Never met him."

"He's swell people, Vanner, but——"

"He wouldn't approve of his son, heir, and Argentine representative getting mixed up in a murder case?" suggested Rick.

"Well, I did get in a hell of a lot of scrapes when I was in school—and after. And he'd bawl the bejesus out of me and get me out of them. Then when I was demobbed, he was tickled pink with the spaghetti. A couple of weeks after I was out I went on a binge one night with some of the gang, and we got in a mess and smashed up a car and Christ all.

"I suppose I'd never thought about it before. Dad didn't say anything, as he would have done in the old times. But there was disappointment in his face. Made me feel pretty cheap. This job was open at the time and I talked him into sending me. At the beginning I made a sweet muddle of a good many things. My college Spanish wasn't much good. I didn't know the ropes. But eventually I got the hang of it. And I'm doing a good job down here, if I do say so myself. And the old man's fit to bust with pride. I flew up for a couple of weeks over Easter, and he radiated pride like an incandescent bulb. It was embarrassing. He's getting on, you know. Seventy, last birthday. And his blood pressure's fluky. And if he sees this, he'll figure——" He stopped. "Skip it. Let's have another drink."

They ordered it. Rick made no comment. After a while he said, "Can you tell me anything about this drive of yours last night, or this morning, rather? Didn't you knock over any old ladies or run into any *colectivos* or even run down a cow or a chicken?"

"Old ladies are home and in bed at that hour. If I'd run

into a *colectivo*, I wouldn't be here now. They always win. And the cows and chickens kept out of my way."

"Where did you go?"

"I headed out through Olivos. Just by chance," Sales added hastily.

"That's where Mantle lives, isn't it?"

Steve looked a bit sheepish. "All right, damnit. I drove by their house."

"See anything interesting?" Rick said it idly, but the instant tension and overquick reply of "No, of course not" made him say, "You evidently did."

"What could I see interesting?"

"Search me. Somebody meeting someone else. Someone arriving at or leaving the house."

"What are you getting at?"

"You quite evidently saw something and you don't want to tell me because you think it may be awkward for Anne."

"It wasn't Anne."

"Mantle?" Rick didn't wait for confirmation or denial but asked, "What was he doing?"

"Driving in."

"Alone?"

"Yes. Driving himself. I've never seen him drive himself before."

"Where'd he come from?"

"Can't tell. He'd turned into their road before I noticed the car." Sales finished his drink and said, "I'm sure there's some simple explanation of it."

"He didn't give it to the police, then," remarked Rick. "We'd better eat. The *maître* has been signaling that our table is waiting since two drinks back."

After lunch Rick borrowed Sales's car and drove to Calle Bartolomé Mitre, where Fred Elting's office was. He had never given much serious thought to the parking problem in the center of Buenos Aires before. He did now. After he'd narrowly missed arrest and destruction several times, he reached the office and found *subjefe* Boggia sitting at the desk, glaring at the papers which were spread around him. Two terrified-looking clerks, one very short and fat and the other very tall and thin, were standing in front of him, quaking visibly each time he lifted his glare from the papers to them.

At the sight of Vanner, Boggia exploded and talked without the apparent need to stop for breath for almost five minutes, ending up with the flat statement that the late Señor Elting had been a *"sin vergüenza"* and a *"canalla"*—meaning a shameless one and a scoundrel. It seemed that the papers in front of him revealed a series of deals and bribes that had shocked even Señor Boggia, used as he was to such occurrences.

Vanner sat down and looked at some of the documents that had so aroused the *subjefe's* ire. Elting had been the Argentine agent for a surprising number of small American companies, but even a cursory glance through his books showed that most of his money had come from activities on the side, giving rise to speculation as to how much more money he might have made which did not show in the books at all. His main source of income seemed to have come from buying large quantities of a worthless stock of a company which suddenly got, or seemed about to get, a government concession, thus causing the stock to rise. In every case the concession was either canceled or refused

97

shortly after, but not before Mr. Elting had sold at profits ranging from 80 per cent to 320 per cent.

"Perhaps we are mistaken and the murder of this *canalla* is not connected with the Deschamps affair. Often deals like this lead to murder."

Vanner agreed that they were not inclined to make people popular.

"On the other hand," said Boggia, "we found this."

"This" was a letter from the Ministerio de Hacienda, signed by a high official, which read, in part, "As regards the other matter, it has already been attended to, and you may rest assured that the Salsa Sales de Argentina, S.A., will not be granted permission to extend their holdings in the direction of the river." It was dated five months before.

"Why should Sales wait until last night?" asked Rick. "Is it your theory that he got the idea from the murder of Deschamps? Sort of infection?"

"The second murder is always easier than the first," said Boggia sententiously.

"You think he just decided that last night was his night to murder? Or, having managed to kill one, he thought it a pity not to keep on killing?" Rick shook his head. "No, Señor Boggia."

The Canning house in Olivos stood back from the road in an attractive garden and two spaniels came out to inspect Rick. They decided they approved as he told a neatly uniformed maid that he would like to speak to Mrs. Canning. While he waited in the paneled hall he heard her voice from the living room, sharp with a mixture of irritation and tears. "Why shouldn't I hurt him? He's hurt me."

A lower voice replied, and Rick couldn't hear it. Then Gloria's came again: "Love! He never did love me. All he wanted was something good-looking and guaranteed English to sit at the head of his table." Again the lower voice spoke, and Gloria replied, "You don't understand. You never did. I don't want to live and die like a vegetable." There was a flurry of footsteps and Gloria ran across the hall, nearly skidded on the parquet flooring at the corner of the stairs, recovered herself, and ran up.

Rick didn't wait for the reappearance of the maid. He walked up to the wide arch from which Gloria had issued. The maid was still standing, looking rather helplessly from the card he had given her to a little old lady who was turned away from her. She saw Rick, looked from the old lady's back to him, then down at the card, then decided to give the whole thing up. She just disappeared back into the hall.

This must be Gloria's mother, to whom she had referred, thought Rick, and coughed. It had no effect. He went over toward her and said, "Excuse me, madame——"

She turned with a little gasp, and a pair of very blue eyes, swimming in tears, looked up at him. She made a tired little gesture and said, "I'm sorry—I didn't——"

He handed her a handkerchief and said, "Come and sit down by the fire." He steered her to an armchair by the open fireplace. "You're English, aren't you? Wouldn't you like a cup of tea?"

From the midst of his handkerchief she said, "The maids don't understand me."

Rick rang the bell he saw by the side of the mantelpiece. The maid returned rather timidly and looked relieved when he ordered tea.

99

He put another log on the fire and sat down. He took the presence of innumerable ash trays as a tacit permission to smoke and lighted a cigarette. He didn't talk. There must have been a kettle boiling in the kitchen, to judge by the speed with which the tea arrived. He motioned to the maid to put it beside him and poured out a cup. "Milk or lemon? And how many sugars?"

"Milk, please, and two lumps." He handed her the cup. She said, "Please forgive me. Old people cry easily, you know. You mustn't pay any attention to me."

"You're not happy here?"

"Gloria is unhappy. I thought it would help her, for me to come. But I seem to have made everything worse." She faltered. Then it dawned on her that she had never seen this large stranger before, that she had no idea who he was.

"Richard Vanner," he answered her question. "I'm a detective and I'm investigating the death of Henri Deschamps."

"But Gloria couldn't tell you anything about that."

He smiled and ignored the remark. "Perhaps you can help me. Did you hear them come in last night?" A shadow across the wrinkled face made him say, "Did something happen?"

"They were quarreling. I could hear them from my room."

"What about?"

She shook her head. "I don't know. Then Gloria came up to her room and Douglas went out. I knocked on Gloria's door, but she'd locked it. She wouldn't let me in." The quiet heartbreak in her voice made Rick wince.

"She's an only daughter?"

The old lady nodded. "I had another—Beatrice—but she died when she was a week old. We wanted Gloria to have a companion, but——"

"How d'you know Douglas went out again last night?"

"I heard the front door open and close and then the car drive off."

"Did you hear him come back?"

She nodded, but before he had time to ask her how long Canning had been absent, Gloria came hurrying in, having done repairs to her make-up and looking radiant. She greeted Rick gaily. "Good afternoon, Sherlock. Did you find out all Mother's sticky secrets? I know she's got a past, but she won't tell me about it. Mother, did you know he's a frightfully important detective? He gets sent round by all the big companies when they have trouble anywhere. The mere fact that the villains know he's coming makes them run for cover."

"Trouble is they sometimes go to cover a bit too deep," remarked Vanner, "and then it's a nuisance flushing them."

Gloria looked at the tea things and said, "Mother, couldn't you do better by our Sherlock than tea?"

"My dear, with your servants, I'm completely dependent on whoever is here to do the ordering." The old lady had recovered a bit. "Mr. Vanner seems like a very sensible and capable man. He ordered my tea for me, and I'm sure he'd have ordered himself something if he'd wanted it."

"What brought you out here?" asked Gloria. "Not a desire for tea, I take it."

"A desire for knowledge."

"About . . . ?"

"Henri Deschamps."

Gloria looked a bit uneasily at her mother and said, "Come over to the bar and I'll tell you what little I know about Henri and give you something a bit stronger than tea."

Her mother got up. "You two stay here by the fire with your drinks. I'm going to my room. You were very kind, Mr. Vanner. Good-by."

Gloria went and mixed two strong whisky and sodas and handed them to Rick. He didn't speak until he had deposited one on each side table by the two armchairs.

"What makes you think I can tell you anything about Henri?" she asked.

"You knew him well."

"You've been listening to some of the gossip around. If you knew more about Buenos Aires, you wouldn't pay any attention to it. Here if one speaks to a man, one is supposed to be living with him, and if one is seen with a woman, one's a Lesbian. Two men dine together and they are inevitably fairies. I'm sick of it."

"It rather depends where one speaks to a man, the conclusions people draw," remarked Rick.

Her blue eyes were watching him shrewdly. "Meaning just what?"

"If one picks an *amueblado* for one's conversations, it's apt to give rise to—shall we say—conclusions?"

A flush rose up her neck. "What d'you mean?"

"You were seen going to one—the Ultra Chic, I think—yesterday afternoon, with Deschamps."

For a moment she looked completely stunned. Then she suddenly jumped to her feet. "If you've said a word of your ideas to Mother, I think I'll——" She stopped, her eyes blazing.

"What?" queried Rick with some amusement.

"I think I'll kill you."

"Better be careful about threatening people. It's so awkward if they turn up dead later."

"What did you say to her?"

"About Deschamps? Nothing. She seemed unhappy enough without that."

"You bloody swine!" She slapped him across the face, hard. He laughed and caught her wrist.

"Are you going to sit down like a good little girl or do I have to put you over my knee?"

For a moment she struggled in silent fury to free herself, then realized the uselessness of it. The fight went out of her. She said dully, "I suppose I asked for it."

"You'd better tell me."

"It isn't as bad as it sounds. We—we weren't taking anything away from Douglas. At least, not anything he wanted. If he'd minded——"

"Does he know?"

She shook her head, then looked up in alarm. "Why? D'you think—— Sometimes I've wondered. But that's just it. He didn't seem to care. He'd just say, 'Go out and amuse yourself, my dear, with a reasonable degree of discretion, of course,' in that sardonic way of his."

"What d'you expect him to do? Beat you? It's out of date."

"Can't you see it from my side at all? Dumped down here among a bunch of cats most of whom made up their minds to dislike me before I arrived, and when they got a look at

103

me they loathed me. I'd committed two unforgivable sins. I'd married one of their eligible males who makes good money and I was better-looking than they were."

"You must be used to having women jealous of you," said Vanner, looking at the shining hair and the fair, clear skin.

"Nothing like the women here," she said bitterly. "I met all Douglas's cronies. I know what they say. 'Doug's a good scout. Of course none of his friends like his wife. Such a pity.' And Douglas was always saying, 'Can't you make friends with some of the women?'"

"Did you ever try?" asked Rick.

"I did, at first. Anyway, it was their business to be friendly to me," she protested. "I was the newcomer. I got on all right with the men."

"I can imagine that," said Rick dryly. "Too well for the women's liking, most probably."

"I did try at first. Honest I did. Oh, what's the use of trying to explain it to a man? You all seem to think that if you stick a woman in a house, give her clothes to wear and a maid to wait on her, that's all she wants. Then you spend all the day at the office, half the evening supervising a boys' club, and when you want her to entertain your friends, she's there, handy. Douglas didn't seem even——" She stopped and then went on again. "I don't know. It's all such a mess. He still has so much trouble with his leg. He always will have. And I'm awfully sorry for him, but——"

"But you're not interested in being a nurse?" suggested Rick.

She flushed again. "That's not fair. Douglas won't let me be. When it's giving him trouble he goes off to his room and says, 'Leave me alone. For God's sake go on to the party and break a few hearts.' As if I were a—I don't know——"

"It could be that he doesn't want to spoil your evening or deprive you of any fun."

"But it's as if I didn't mean anything, like a—like a——" She gave up the search for a simile and finished her drink.

Rick wondered if they were ever going to get to Henri Deschamps. If ever he wanted to change his profession, he thought, he ought to become a padre; he had sufficient experience in hearing confessions. He had occasionally looked at his own face in a mirror to try to discover what there was in it that caused people to tell him their troubles, their pasts, and their dreams for the future. With a view to keeping the flow going in the hope that it might eventually lead to Deschamps, and remembering the glimpse of Canning's twisted face as he had got up from his chair once the night before, he said, "I think your husband suffers a good deal, and I know if I'm in pain, all I want is to be left alone."

Genuine surprise was in her blue eyes. "But if you loved someone, you'd want them to be there."

"Not unless they happened to be armed with a morphine pill or something useful."

"Henri once said——" she began. "I forget exactly, but it was something like that."

"He probably knew. Did you meet him when he first came down here from Rio?"

"He hadn't been here very long. I saw him round at parties. I'd heard stories about him, but I thought——" She gave a dreary little laugh. "Women are such fools. They always think it will be different. They know how a man's treated the ones before them. You *know* he'll give you the same deal, but you close your eyes to it. Henri always had ideas about somewhere to go or something to do. He made me feel as if I were important to him, even though, down inside, I knew it wouldn't last. That was at the beginning."

"And then . . . ?" prompted Rick.

"I knew he was taking Anne out a lot, but from something Douglas had said, I knew Mantle didn't approve and I didn't think she'd go against his wishes. She adores her uncle, you know. And then I saw the announcement in the paper. I tried to get hold of Henri, but he avoided me. It made me furious. At least he could have told me himself instead of letting me read it in the paper.

"I saw him at the Watsons' cocktail party and told him I'd got to talk to him. We made a date for yesterday. We couldn't go to the apartment because of his sister. So he picked me up at Retiro. He seemed to take it all as a matter of course. He said, 'But haven't we amused each other?' I could have killed him for saying that."

"Because it was true?"

"No, it wasn't. Oh, I don't know. Perhaps it was true in a way. But it made me feel like a——"

"So you had a quarrel?" prompted Rick when she didn't go on.

Suddenly the trend of his questions dawned on her. "But I didn't kill him," she said quickly.

"You'd just have liked to have done."

"I don't think even that. I don't know. When first someone said he was dead, I thought I was glad, but——"

A little later he asked, "Have you remembered any more details about whom you were talking to after dinner?"

"No. I went with Louise to the little girls' room. They'd turned on the radio to get the fight. Prize fights bore me. I never understand a word the Spanish announcers are saying, and Douglas shushes me every time I say anything. And then Dot Vidal came into the bedroom and started being sweetly acid about the play tonight."

"Where were the people when you came back?"

"Bob was still at the bar. And——" She suddenly stopped dead. Her head was turned away as she continued, hurriedly, "I drifted over and sat down by Arrietti, as far from the radio as I could get. He was dull. He always is. He seemed worried about something."

"Who was missing?"

"I don't remember noticing if anyone was." She turned and faced him. "Come to think of it, I don't remember noticing you. But then I didn't really look."

"I'm crushed," he told her.

"I hadn't noticed you paying any great attention to me."

"Considering the moderate quantity that had been drunk, it's amazing how little people remember—or say they remember," remarked Rick, and got up.

The fear swept back across her face. "There's something you haven't told me."

"What?"

"How you found out?"

"From someone who won't talk."

"I must know. Who?"

"Trust my judgment."

"Mother——" Gloria was looking into the fire. "She has different ideas from ours. She's another generation. She doesn't understand."

The man smiled a little. "I think your mother understands a good deal more than you, Gloria."

"They thought differently about these things." There was a kind of defensive desperation in her voice. She looked up into his face. His gray eyes looked tired, she thought, but they didn't condemn; they looked as if they had seen too much. She said in what was scarcely more than a whisper, "I don't want her to know."

"She won't learn from me."

CHAPTER 8

As he drove toward the Mantle house, which was also in
Olivos, Rick pondered the evasions in Gloria's story. Super-
ficially the pattern was obvious. But underneath it went
deeper. She was beautiful, but unsure of herself. She needed
someone to tell her she was loved, that she was wanted, that
she was necessary. Probably Canning hadn't known many
people in England and had given all his time to her. Then
when he came back here he had had his own interests, his
business, his boys' club, his old friends. And she, on her side,
was away from all her friends, a stranger to his circle, all of
whom would look with hypercritical eyes at the newcomer
and especially such a striking-looking newcomer. It was all
very natural and inevitable.

Perhaps his preoccupation with Gloria and her problem
was the reason that he got lost twice en route to the Mantle
house, which was only three squares away. A manservant
opened the door, and then a housekeeper came into the hall
to speak to him. "If you're another reporter, the door is

behind you," was her theme song. Rick explained himself.

"I don't think the Señorita Anne should see you." The good lady looked worried. "But I don't know what to do with her. She's insisting on appearing in this play tonight if they can't find a substitute. I think it's indecent. But she says they've put a lot into the production and she can't let them down. If she's going to appear in the play, I don't know why she shouldn't interview you."

In due course Anne appeared. She looked tired and listless. "Of course I remember you, Mr. Vanner. Someone told me you were a detective."

"It's one of a detective's unpleasant jobs, Miss Mantle, to have to bother people at a time like this," Vanner told her. "But I am sure that you, more than anyone else, want to arrive at the truth about it."

"It still seems so impossible. Henri was so lighthearted. He couldn't hurt anyone."

"Sometimes it's the lighthearted people who do," replied Rick, marveling at how greatly she had failed to understand the man she was going to marry. "They don't mean to, but they do."

"You mean women?"

"Could be."

"When Henri first used to take me out I always used to say to him, 'What number am I in the series, Henri?' I'd heard all the stories, you see. I never took him seriously for a long time—until——"

Rick did not pursue the subject. "Did he ever mention enemies?"

"No."

"Your uncle didn't approve of the match?"

She shook her head and after a while said, "It was the one thing that worried me."

"What did he give as his reasons?"

"His reasons were . . ." She fumbled for a word. "It was so unlike Uncle. He is usually so explicit about everything. But he wasn't, about this. Once he said, 'Henri is an old man.' And he was thirty-four. And I told Uncle, 'That isn't old.' 'All the same, he is an old man,' he said. 'There is too much of a gap between what you've known and understood and what is behind him for you to be happy.' Another thing I think Uncle thought—that Henri knew Uncle—that I—I mean, if anything happens to Uncle, I'd get the company. I told Henri I was afraid Uncle thought that, and he just laughed, the way he always did, and said, '*Eh bien,* and I will retire from the diplomatic service and live on my rich wife!' " The tears came up in her eyes as she said it.

"I know what your uncle meant about his being old," Rick said slowly.

"I know too. He'd been in concentration camp. He'd had to do things which I've never had to do. I understand that." She lifted her clear young face which, even now, had so little but faith and blind courage written on it. "And Justine said something which I think is true. She said, 'There is a wonderful healing power in forgetfulness, and he can only forget with people who had not had the same experiences.' "

"She was looking at it from her brother's point of view. It's true, of course. But it's sometimes a bit tough on the other person."

"You don't expect marriage to be a complete bed of roses."

Rick didn't answer. "Try to remember who was sitting where and if they got up and disappeared or anything like that during the fifteen minutes before Sales and Canning found him."

"Mr. Vanner"—she leaned forward earnestly—"I'm sure Steve didn't have anything to do with it. I hadn't realized until someone said something, just as we were leaving last night, that that was what some people thought. Steve couldn't do a thing like that. I'm terribly fond of Steve. I know him. He couldn't do a thing like that. He just *couldn't*."

"So far the *argumentum ad hominem* is all we have in his favor."

"I'd trust Steve anywhere or anyhow. He'd never let you down."

"We'd better try to find some evidence to help him," Rick reminded her. "Did Henri say anything to you about any of the people there last night?"

"He asked some questions about you, as a matter of fact, and we had to get Louise to supply the information. That's how I knew you were a detective and had been in the Intelligence. He said Elting was a '*salaud*' and wondered why the Farehams put up with him. I asked him what was the matter with Elting and he said 'I'll tell you sometime when we've got all night. It would take all night.'"

"Anybody else?"

"He asked who Fresne was. He'd never met him before."

"Anything special he wanted to know about him?"

"What he did, how long he'd been in the country. Just the ordinary sort of thing."

"D'you remember whom Henri talked to before dinner?"

"To me, mostly. And Uncle. He seemed a bit absent-minded."

"How?"

"I don't know. It was just an idea of mine. I said something to him and he asked me to repeat it, and when I teased him about not listening, he said, 'Sorry, I was thinking of something else.' And I was worried."

"Because he hadn't been paying attention?"

"Good heavens, no! But I hadn't had a chance to talk to him except on the phone since I'd met Justine, and I did want her to like me. Henri thought an awful lot of her, you know. And I was afraid she—well, you never know how families will feel about prospective brides."

"So he seemed absent-minded before dinner? Right away when he arrived or after he'd talked to someone there?"

"I thought maybe it was because of Gloria Canning being there. At one time there'd been gossip about him and Gloria."

"And after dinner?"

"I sat near the radio for a while. Henri stood near me for a minute or two, then Elting came and leaned against the radio. Henri went and spoke to Justine and asked me if I wanted a liqueur. Then I went along to Louise's room."

"You hadn't noticed where Henri went after he asked if you wanted a liqueur?"

She shook her head miserably. "Toward the little bar, I think, but I'm not sure."

"That is by the door. But you don't remember passing him on your way out?"

"I'm sure I didn't. I mean, I'd have known if I had."

"Did he ever tell you he thought he was being followed?"

"Followed? No." She looked her question, but he didn't choose to notice it.

A maid came down and set a suitcase in the hall. She said, "I've packed everything, señorita."

"For the play tonight," Anne explained. She got up and stood with her back turned to him. "People are so difficult. I don't want to do the play, but when they called I said I would if they couldn't get anybody else. It's too late to get someone new. It's only a small part, the maid; it's *Blithe Spirit*, you know. But she comes on and off a lot. We had the dress rehearsal on Sunday and there isn't time. And I only said I'd do it so as not to let them down, and now several people have made it quite clear they think it's heartless. They've all advised me not to." It ended on a sniff.

Rick smiled. "There's a Spanish proverb, 'Don't give me advice; I can make my own mistakes.' One can't allow one's private grief to dislocate everyone else."

"They've spent so much money and time on it, it seemed unfair to let them down. Justine understood."

Again the man smiled. "Mme. Trinquard is very wise."

"I don't mind what people think about me, but I'd hate them to think that Henri hadn't——" She disappeared into the handkerchief. "You must think me an awful fool" came from its depths. The sound of a car in the drive made her look up. "Oh dear. That'll be Justine, and I don't want her to—I mean, it's hard enough for her as it is."

"You go up and powder your nose. I'll talk to Mme. Trinquard for a moment."

"You must have made an awfully nice brother for some girl," she sniffed as she got up.

"Thanks for not saying 'father.'"

As she ran up the stairs, Rick went out into the hall. The moment he saw Justine Trinquard get out of the car he knew something was wrong. The big Basque chauffeur put out a hand to steady her. He looked worried. Rick went forward. "What's happened?"

"Where's Anne?" The woman's face was gray and filmed with sweat.

"Upstairs. She'll be down in a minute."

"Someone took a shot at me. I don't want Anne frightened."

The chauffeur came, still looking worried. Rick got a hold of Justine's arm and led her in.

She went on. "As I came out of the building. Man from a car opposite. I thought it best to come on here. Domingo promised to say nothing." She sat very gratefully in the chair to which he piloted her.

"How bad is it?" asked Rick. He had gone to the little bar and already found and poured a slug of brandy.

"Nothing. I put a scarf——"

He brought her the brandy. She drank it in a gulp. He opened her coat. The blouse was stained, the buttons undone. He pushed it aside and found a white silk scarf wedged on the left side. "Hm. Pretty deep furrow. Ribs okay?" As he said it he was thinking that a half inch to the right and it would have been a different story. He heard Anne's footsteps on the stairs and rebuttoned her coat. "Leave this to me."

Anne came in. "Justine dear, I'm so sorry. I was just seeing your room was ready."

"And after being up all night with the police going over the apartment, it's about all you're fit for," said Rick lightly.

"Listen to Doc Vanner. We're going to take your guest right upstairs, Anne, and make her lie down. But I do have to bother her with a few questions."

"Of course. Anything I can do to help." The brandy had made the grayness recede from Justine's face.

"Mr. Vanner!" It was a protest from Anne. "She's tired to death."

"I would like to lie down, but M. Vanner's questions won't bother me." Justine got up fairly steadily.

"It's all wrong," said Anne.

It seemed quite natural that Rick should go upstairs with them. A manservant had already taken the bag. Justine threw her hat onto the dressing table. Rick helped her off with her topcoat, carefully, but in spite of that, he knew it hurt.

"Why don't you go to bed?" said Anne.

"I'll just lie down like this for a while and answer M. Vanner's questions, and then later, maybe, I'll sleep a bit if you don't mind."

A bit unwillingly, Anne went; she paused in the doorway. "Anything I can get you?"

"Not now, thanks."

When she'd closed the door, Rick said, "Let me look at that properly. It may need a doctor."

Justine shook her head. "In my bag. Iodine, bandage, adhesive." She gave a faint smile. "I always travel with them. Pocket on the right-hand side."

He found them and came back. She'd undone the coat and blouse. He pulled out the scarf. The furrow had gone down the side of the left breast. "It's clean," he said. Fingers which were by no means inexperienced were feeling the rib. "But you should have an X-ray."

"Later, perhaps. Vanner, I couldn't face another session of police questions. It—I can't stand it."

"I know." He was working quite expertly. "How much of a look did you get at the man?"

"Hardly a glimpse. He leaned out of the car window. Hat pulled down. I ducked into the car and told Domingo to get going. He was more than willing."

"What kind of car was it?"

"American. I think a Buick. Quite old. I did not get the number."

"And you'd never seen the man who shot before?"

"No. His hat was well pulled down," she repeated, "and I think he had a trenchcoat. It looked like the collar of one, turned up."

"Who else knew you were leaving to come down here besides Anne, Mantle, myself, the chauffeur, and Fresne?"

"The Embassy. I'd told them in case they wanted to find me. Also the maid, Dolores."

Rick finished what he was doing with adhesive tape. "One rib is broken, and that is a makeshift job," he said. "You really should have a doctor."

"And that means police and questions——" For a second a fleeting horror was in her eyes.

"Okay. I understand," he said. "I'll attend to the police. One more thing. The only reason for this attempt is that the murderer is afraid you know something. Are you quite sure there is nothing you've half forgotten?"

"D'you think I haven't been asking myself that? I can't think of anything."

117

When he got downstairs he said to Anne, "She didn't get any sleep last night with the police ransacking the apartment, and she's dead-beat. All she needs is rest."

There were several things that Rick wanted to do when he got back to the center of town, but as he couldn't do them all at once, he went first to an old-fashioned office in Calle San Martin, the door of which bore the legend: JORGE SEMINARIO—*Inquiries—commercial—private—handled with expedition and precision.*

The private detective heaved his bulk from behind his worn desk and said, "You have two murders to solve now, I hear. Your friend Mr. Sales is unfortunate. Or guilty."

"Unfortunate," said Rick, and sat down. "What have you got for me?"

"Here's the past history of the people you asked for. Not all complete yet." Seminario pushed a thick folder toward him. "D'you think the motive for the killing lies in the past?"

"Doubt it. But I want to know something about the people."

Rick skipped through the Farehams, knowing their history through friends in New York. The report on Dorothy Vidal did not tell him as much as he had learned from the French Embassy, except to supply a long list of amateur theatricals in which she had appeared. Nor was the history of Dr. Arrietti interesting; he seemed to have studied in a large number of universities and hold an impsosing number of degrees, but that was all.

The late Fred Elting's past went only as far back as 1944, when he had arrived in Buenos Aires with a vague United States government job connected with the purchase of raw materials. He had entertained on a large scale, lived at the Alvear Palace Hotel, and a year later the government had felt that his expenses were excessive compared to the results and he had been recalled. Having made a number of business connections, he returned in 1946 with the agencies for a number of firms. The list followed. He'd married a girl who worked in the United States Embassy and maintained a *garçonnière* in Calle Parana. He had been involved in an investigation concerning fifty thousand American cigarettes which had arrived in the country without the formality of an exchange order, and his name had also been mentioned in connection with some Swiss watches which had also come in without benefit of red tape. Neither charge had been proved.

Rick turned to the Cannings next and learned nothing that he had not known before. The thickest sheaf was devoted to Howard Mantle, and Vanner settled back in his chair to peruse it. Seminario's man had made a thorough job. Attached were newspaper clippings about the killing of Mantle's partner, Walter Downs, in 1922, at which time Mantle's younger brother, Hugh, was also a member of the firm.

On September 10, 1922, Adorna Anetto, Mantle's secretary, was found dead in her room; the autopsy showed that she was two months pregnant. The following day the office staff heard a quarrel between Mantle and Downs. As there had been frequent quarrels between the two men and it was an open secret that Mantle wanted to buy Downs out, they did not pay much attention, but Downs was heard to say, "When I tell what I know, you'll have a surprise." The staff left at six-thirty. Mantle and Downs

remained working in their separate offices. When a cleaning woman came at nine o'clock, she found Downs shot
through the head with Mantle's gun.

Mantle claimed not to have seen or spoken to Downs
after the quarrel, not to have heard a shot, and to have left
at about ten to seven, at which time he stated he presumed
Downs was still alive. The police were never able to shake
his story.

He had taken over the business, and in the intervening
years built it up into the colossal Mantex Company. Hugh
Mantle had started a jam factory with another Englishman.
It had not been a success, and at the time of his death in a
railway accident between Bahia Blanca and Buenos Aires,
in 1938, he had been heavily in debt.

Howard Mantle had paid up his debts and fetched Anne,
who had then been in school in Switzerland, and taken her
to the United States and arranged for her to finish her edu-
cation there.

Vanner read over the story of the killing of Downs
several times. A porter had noticed Mantle leave and agreed
that it might have been ten to seven, but he couldn't say for
sure. The damning fact remained that no one admitted
seeing Downs alive after the staff left at six-thirty. It was
impossible to prove that no one had visited the office later,
but it was equally impossible to prove that anyone had.

Attached was a clipping recording the death of the porter, in 1925, in Salta, where he had bought a small farm. He
had, it appeared, retired a few months after the murder,
which was suggestive. Another sheet gave the history of
the Mantex Company, the expansions, the stock issue, and

present capitalization. Howard Mantle appeared to be a nice blend of financial genius and ruthlessness.

Finally Rick passed on to Michel Fresne. Born 1899 in Nantes, France. Arrived in Buenos Aires from Lisbon, September 14, 1945. Went into partnership with a Swiss called Gaston Duame in a real-estate venture, but less than six months later this association was dissolved and Fresne set up for himself. He had an office in Avenida de Mayo and was registered as an importer and exporter. He also had a *depósito* on Calle Pedro Mendoza. He employed three male clerks and was thought to handle job lots of merchandise. His apartment was on Charcas and he banked with the Bank of Boston. He was not registered at the French Consulate, who could give no information about him.

Rick grunted and pushed the papers away from him. "What d'you remember about the Downs killing?" he asked.

Seminario rubbed the top of his head and squinted at the ceiling. "I've been thinking about it this afternoon. The porter was undoubtedly fixed. Or why did he retire so shortly afterward? He was quite a young man. Only fifty-two when he died. Means he was forty-eight when he retired. And in those days you didn't make enough money as a porter to retire at forty-eight. Lord knows now, with these barbarous new laws, everybody will be retiring at twenty-five, if they manage to do any work until then." Rick smiled, and though Seminario was still looking at the ceiling, he noticed it. "All very well for you to grin. I've got a man now who's no use to prop up a wall, but I can't afford to fire him. He's been with me for fourteen years. I'd have to pay him a month's salary for every year's service, plus his separation money. It's cheaper to keep him on the pay roll."

"I've heard a lot of people say the same thing," said Rick.

"Another thing"—Seminario went back to the murder— "Mantle is a clever man. After the whole office staff, including his own brother, had heard this row, he wouldn't have been such a fool as to kill Downs like that. He'd have hired it done or got him out into the country or shot him on a dark night or something."

"Perhaps he was in a hurry. What is it Downs was supposed to have said? 'When I tell what I know, you'll have a surprise.' One of the clerks said he heard that. No. Two of them. Wonder why the brother didn't hear it if he was still there."

"Probably did but did not want to testify against his brother," said Seminario. "I believe Howard had done a lot for him."

"Um. What was the general theory as to what Downs meant when he said that?"

"*Dios!* It's twenty-six years ago! People said that Howard was responsible for the girl's condition, that he wouldn't marry her, and as she lived at home with strict parents, she had committed suicide."

"If he was responsible for the girl's condition, it would hardly be a surprise to him," objected Rick.

"Might be a surprise that Downs knew it."

"How did Mantle explain it?"

"He didn't. He just refused to answer." Seminario paused and added, "Another theory was that Hugh was responsible and Howard killed Downs to cover him."

"Odd how little seems to be known about the Señores Elting and Fresne before they came here."

"Probably isn't creditable whatever it is," snorted Seminario. "I don't know what our immigration authorities are doing. They seem to let in all the scallywags of Europe and North America."

"Our red tape is just the same," Rick consoled him. "We give every would-be immigrant forms miles long and demand God knows how many guarantees, but a very fine assortment of crooks manages to get in just the same." Rick was looking through the preliminary reports on what the people had been doing during the day. So far, nobody had done anything worth investigating.

"It might interest you to know." remarked Seminario, "that my boy who went over to the police to get the précis of the Mantle case found out that someone else had been looking it up within the last month. The official in charge of the records told him."

"Did he say who it was?"

"Esteban Morales. The remarkable thing is that Esteban is a cousin of M. Mars's wife and often does jobs for him."

"Mars! Well, I'll be damned."

"Ah—you know M. Mars."

"I know who he is."

"I can give you his home address if he is not at the Embassy," said Seminario, playing with his watch chain.

A few minutes later Rick got up. "Keep tails on Douglas and Gloria Canning. Mantle. Fresne. Vidal."

"It's going to cost something. They all have cars, and Mantle and the Cannings live outside."

"I think it'll be worth it." He produced from his pocket

the paper on which he'd written down the addresses of which Deschamps had made a note. "Send a man to these addresses and find out if a maid who once worked for Dorothy Vidal lives there. Call me when you get anything."

"I will. But why doesn't your friend, Señor Sales, go to Montevideo for a few days? Charming city. Delightful people."

"Stephen Sales is innocent," said Rick flatly.

"Even so, Montevideo is a charming city." Seminario rubbed his bald spot and gazed at his watch chain.

CHAPTER 9

The porter at the Plaza seemed excited when Rick got back and handed him a fat bunch of telephone calls. It was the one on top that had aroused the porter's excitement. "Call Mr. Jefferson Sales of New York at once. He will pay charges. Worth 2-0089 before five, and after, Rhinelander 4-0028." Vanner read the rest of them in the elevator. Mr. Canning, four times. Mr. Mantle, twice. Mrs. Fareham, twice. Mr. Sales, twice. Mr. Fresne, only once. The American Consulate, twice. The French Embassy.

Quite a satisfactory amount of interest, he reflected as he went into his room. He put in the New York call and then busied himself about the others. Mr. Canning wanted to talk to him but not on the phone. Could Mr. Vanner come to his office? No, he couldn't. Then Mr. Canning would come to the hotel.

Mantle's line was busy, so he called the Consulate, and was given another number to call. "I told you old man Sales would be on the warpath, and he is," said the consul's harassed voice. "Been on the phone from New York, and he's done something to the State Department so they've been on the phone too."

"He called me," said Rick.

"He's liable to get a plane and come down here, and then he'll get us all in the soup."

"I'll try and stave him off."

"Anything new?"

"Lots. But it doesn't make much sense yet."

"Let me know when you've anything I can pass on to keep 'em all quiet. The ambassador's been on my neck as well."

"If he thinks murders get solved in twenty-four hours, I wish he'd come along and solve it," growled Rick.

"I wish you'd tell him that."

"I probably will, if he gets after me. I'm not always famous for my tact. Hold the fort, and I'll do my best to send you some ammunition."

He called Mantle back and got him. Mr. Mantle also wanted to talk, but not on the phone. " I could stop by your hotel. I have to be early because of this damned play."

"I was thinking of going," said Rick, "in which case I'll see you there."

"Not a very good spot for private conversation," said Mantle.

"Someone's coming over here in a few minutes and I don't know how long they'll stay, and I'm waiting for a long-distance call. How about tomorrow morning, at your office? As early as you like. Or stop by here on your way in."

There was an infinitesimal pause at the other end. Howard Mantle was not used to having his wishes ignored.

When he summoned people they came. Then he said, "I'll stop in on my way at your hotel and call upstairs. If you're free, perhaps you'll spare me a minute."

"With pleasure."

Mrs. Fareham was next. "I heard you were investigating. Have you found anything? I feel awful. About it happening in our house. One sort of feels as if—— And the reporters have been driving me mad. I don't know what to say to them. I've just given up and told them it isn't in the least my idea of a novelty in the entertainment line. Murder with the liqueurs.

"And it's going to be ghastly at the play tonight. You know it's *Blithe Spirit*, and that's not a very helpful subject in the circumstances. And everybody will expect Bob and me to provide some gory details, and I've told Bob we should have diplomatic colds and he said we have to go. Have you found out anything? I'm sure Steve Sales didn't do it. I knew his mother. Ages ago."

"Just tell all the curious that the next time you arrange a murder you'll save them a front seat," suggested Rick. "And we must warn Steve when he finds bodies scattered around at dinner parties he must stay well away from them, don't clutch the weapon and yell for help."

"Anyway, thank goodness, you do sound cheerful about it all. That's something. I've been worried sick. His mother was so nice. She's been dead for ages."

Rick forebore from pointing out that his cheerfulness was merely a natural instinct to answer her in the vein in which she had spoken. He said, "There are lots of other candidates for the post of murderer."

"That's a relief. I went to see Justine this morning. It's

ghastly for her. Coming all these miles and having him killed. So I went. But I'm sure she'd much rather have been left in peace. She didn't say so, of course. She was appallingly polite. But I'm sure she was praying I'd go. If I'd been she, I'd have been praying it too. So I did. But one doesn't want her to feel we're heartless."

There was a click on the line and the operator's voice said, "We have your New York call, Mr. Vanner."

"Did we get cut off or something? I'm so jittery since last night I find myself jumping at shadows and looking under beds. And I made Bob stay in my room last night."

"Mrs. Fareham, I have a long-distance call waiting. I'll call you back."

"Why didn't you say so? Good-by. Thanks for calling. See you at the play." She hung up.

Rick waited. He could hear scraps of voices. "New York. Ready with New York. Buenos Aires calling Mr. Jefferson Sales." Then the voice spoke into his ear. "Here's your party, Mr. Vanner."

He said, "Vanner speaking."

"My son tells me you're investigating this murder he's involved in." The voice was a curt growl. "My friends at Standard Oil say you know your business."

"That's why they hire me," Rick replied dryly.

"I want the truth about this. How did he get mixed up in it?"

"By going to a perfectly sedate dinner party where the murder was committed. He found the body."

"The tabloids say his arrest is imminent."

"Possibly. It's a long way from arrest to conviction."

"It's not the first time the boy's been in a scrape." There was a tentative note in the gruff voice.

"The boy's a man now, Mr. Sales, and it isn't a scrape."

"Are you a friend of his?"

"He served under me a short time during the war."

"You know who I am. I'm a rich man. You have carte blanche to bribe or buy him out of any jam."

"I think it can be done legally."

"I'll probably fly to B.A. tomorrow."

"Don't."

"Good God! Why not?" It was a splutter.

"You've upset the Embassy quite enough with long-distance calls and needling the State Department. You'll only make the situation more complicated if you come."

"You're not afraid to state your opinions, Vanner."

"Didn't Standard Oil tell you that?"

"I don't trust the so-called justice in these Latin countries."

"Okay. But don't say so out loud, and particularly don't say so where newspapermen will hear you. They don't like it. So far the police have co-operated with me very well. Don't upset the status quo. And lay off the State Department. Steve doesn't need any protection from his government yet."

"Better have it too soon than too late."

"Why don't you ask 'em to send down the Atlantic Squadron?"

"Well—perhaps you know best." It sounded unwilling. "I believe in hiring a man and giving him a chance to show what he can do."

"Big of you."

"Call me the moment you have news. I'll pay the charges. When will that be?"

"I'm a detective, not a prophet."

"Call me at this time tomorrow and report."

"I'll try."

"Good luck to you."

"Thanks. Good-by."

Rick hung up and said "Phew!" He could see why the consul had sounded harried. He called Steve.

"Rick, my dad's seen the papers and he——" began Sales, Jr.

"I've just had ten minutes of him on the phone."

"He's coming down."

"I tried to talk him out of it."

"Ha! You don't know how funny that is. Dad isn't to be talked out of things when he's made up his mind."

"I told him he'd gum up the works."

"You told him—what?"

"I asked him why he didn't tell them to send the Atlantic Squadron down to rescue you. He got the idea."

"I'll be a ——"

"Probably."

"Look, Rick, I'm supposed to be going to this damned play tonight. It'll be hellish, but I figure if I don't go——"

"Better go. Make mental notes of the people who cut you and get even with them later on. Should be fun."

"Your sense of humor is perverted."

"It needs to be in my business. Why don't you come with me? You'll have to anyway. I've got your car. When and where is the damned thing and how long does it take to get there?"

"About fifteen minutes from my place. The Intimate Theater. It's at nine-thirty."

There was a knock on the door and Rick called out, "Come in," and said to the phone, "I'll pick you up at nine-fifteen."

"I tried to get myself announced," said Douglas Canning as he came in, "but you've been on the phone solidly for the last ten minutes."

"Sit down," said Rick. "Drink?"

"Thanks." Canning eased himself into a chair and watched as Rick poured the drinks. "How's the investigation coming?"

"As well as could be expected at this stage of the game. Say when."

"Thanks. Gloria said you were at the house this afternoon."

"Yes."

"Shouldn't think she could tell you anything. She's not observant."

"One has to check on everything." Rick took a long pull at his drink and took out cigarettes. Canning was the one who had sought the interview and it was up to him to speak his piece.

After some time he said, "Deschamps was a great one for running after the girls."

"Or did they run after him?" queried Rick.

"One was always hearing stories," said Canning vaguely, and there was a long pause. "What's the police theory? That the murderer was lying in wait for him or followed him from the room."

"Could have been either."

"You mean he might have waited in Bob's bedroom."

"Depends on the sex of the murderer. A woman would have attracted attention."

"But it couldn't have been a woman."

"Why not?"

"The blows must have taken some strength."

"Not more than would have been possessed by a normal healthy woman—or by an angry one." Rick let that sink in and then said, "When you went into Bob's room and found the bathroom door locked, why didn't you wait?"

"Didn't want to miss the fight. I used to box a bit."

Rick was silent. Canning finished his drink and put it down. "Well, you're busy. I mustn't keep you. I'll be pushing off."

Vanner got up. "Without saying what you came to say or finding out what you came to find out?"

"What's that?"

"You heard me, Canning. There's something you want to say, but you don't know how much I know."

Canning hadn't risen. He looked up at Rick and his face was white and strained. At last he said. "I wanted to ask you a favor."

"What?"

"The papers can be pretty brutal here. There's been some gossip, about my wife and Deschamps. There's always gossip about a woman as pretty as Gloria, and in a place like this tongues wag overtime. It was all very harmless. She's full of life and loves dancing. He was amusing and danced well. But if the papers get it, they'll make a scandal of it."

Rick made no comment. He said, "Where did you go last night after you'd taken Gloria home?"

Canning opened his mouth as if he were going to say, "How did you find out?" but he didn't say it. "I had some business to attend to. And believe me," he added with a faint smile, "it was not murdering Fred Elting."

"I hope the police will believe you. Why did you take your wife's gloves and put them in your pocket?"

"Gloria's always leaving things."

"You didn't take her evening bag."

"I knew she wouldn't forget that."

"Remarkable, considering how—er—sleepy you were."

A bit unwillingly, Canning said, "Matter of fact, I hadn't slept at all the night before. I don't sometimes."

"Thought out all your answers, haven't you?"

"What d'you mean?"

"D'you think your wife killed Deschamps?"

"Are you raving? Gloria! I'm sure she didn't." He got up with difficulty. "If I weren't a cripple, you wouldn't say that to me."

It was on the tip of Rick's tongue to retort, "If you weren't a cripple, you wouldn't say that to me," but he refrained. The weary bitterness in Canning's face as he turned toward the door hurt. He said "Hell!" and poured some more whisky into the glass and went up to him. "Listen, Canning, I'm not a complete fool. You've come here this evening and told me a pack of—I'll be polite—half-truths and evasions. The sooner you realize that they don't help, the better for you and your wife. Eventually the truth comes out. I've seen a good many more of these cases than you and I know. Good God, man, d'you think it amuses me to harry people? Drink your drink and tell me what you're afraid of."

133

After a momentary hesitation Canning took the glass. "Once you've got the murderer, there won't be any more of this inquisition, will there?"

Rick eyed him narrowly. "If I am satisfied it's the right man or woman."

The telephone rang. Rick picked it up. Mr. Mantle was downstairs. "My visitor is just leaving. Come up in five minutes." He turned back to Canning. "Think it over. There aren't going to be any frame-ups and there aren't going to be any phony confessions, or I'll know the reason why."

Canning was silent, his back to the door. At last he said, "What does it feel like to play God?"

"I wouldn't know. I've never done it." Rick waited. Canning had the door open. "Mantle is on his way up," said Rick.

After Canning had gone, he stood for a half moment in the middle of the room, thinking in terms of lurid profanity. Finally he went and poured himself another drink.

The owner of the Mantex Company looked extraordinarily ill. Ought to run a hospital for this bunch, thought Rick, with a special ward for war neuroses, inferiority complexes, and "nobody loves me" complaints. He pushed forward a chair.

"I'm grateful to you for sparing me a few moments," said Mantle with a slightly sarcastic undercurrent. "I won't keep you long."

"Drink?"

"No, thanks." Unlike Canning, Mantle came straight to the point. "You are probably familiar by now with the story of the murder, twenty-six years ago, of my partner, Walter Downs."

"I am."

"I'd like to ask you a favor." It was said stiffly. Howard Mantle was not used to asking favors. He considered Vanner for a moment and didn't alter the opinion he had formed the night before. This was a good friend and a ruthless enemy; it was not a man you could buy or scare. He went on, "Anne does not know that story. It happened two months before she was born, and she left the Argentine when she was ten, to go to school in Switzerland. She did not come back here to live until three years ago. It's all past history now. I would be obliged to you," he finished with difficulty, "if you don't tell her."

"Why ask me specially out of the two and a half million people in Buenos Aires, or is it three million?"

"I don't think it's very likely that anybody else would mention it," remarked Mantle. "After all, it's hardly social usage to say, 'Your uncle's a murderer.' Particularly," he added cynically, "when he's got as much money as I have."

"It does dictate people's behavior," agreed Rick.

"Anne's had enough of a shock with Deschamps' death. And I——" Mantle stopped and then said, "I know it would distress her." It hadn't been what he had been going to say.

Rick smiled at the ceiling. "I think you underestimate Anne's loyalty and her faith in you."

"What's that got to do with it?"

"If you'd take my advice, which you won't, you'd tell her yourself and as soon as possible."

"You think she's bound to find out?" When Rick didn't answer, he said, "I see."

"Who pensioned off the porter?"

Mantle didn't pretend to misunderstand. He looked squarely at Rick and said, "I did."

"Did the girl leave a note behind when she committed suicide?"

"Yes."

"Did it name the man responsible for the baby?"

"No. Just begged her parents' pardon."

"Her parents didn't know who the man was?"

"No. They credited me."

"Your defense of the case was singularly weak."

"You seem well informed about it."

"Well enough informed to have noticed that."

"The case against me was not proven."

"Not a very satisfactory verdict if you were innocent."

"But better than a prison sentence," answered Mantle with a slight smile.

"The philosophical point of view. I was reading the history of your company, Mantle. It reveals a fighter, ruthless and sometimes not too scrupulous, but essentially a fighter who doesn't know when he's beaten."

"Business here isn't for weaklings."

"That's the point I'm making."

Mantle eyed him shrewdly and said, "All this has nothing to do with my request."

"My professional interest. As to your request, I can assure you that Anne won't learn from me. But I still advise you to tell her."

Mantle said, "Thank you. I'm grateful," and seemed about to get up.

136

"Why didn't you approve of the match between Anne and Deschamps?"

"In my opinion," replied Mantle slowly, "Deschamps was one of those unfortunates left behind after every war whose foundations have been completely upset. I'm not blaming him. God knows, I saw it after the first World War, and this one was ten times worse. I don't know what he went through. But something happened to him that swept away all his values, his faith, his interest in living. I felt him to be incapable of really loving a woman. He had no real belief in the value of making a home and raising children."

"Have you?" inquired Rick when he stopped.

"I'm a man of fifty-eight with no intention of marrying," said Mantle dryly. "The situation is not comparable. I could sympathize with Deschamps, but that doesn't say I thought he was the right husband for Anne. Anne has a right to all the things he couldn't give her. One day she would have known what she had missed.

"To Deschamps, marriage with Anne was suitable, advisable. She attracted him. But he didn't love her. Not with the kind of love Anne is looking for. Then there were his women. That alone wouldn't have prejudiced me. I don't expect a man to be a monk. But there have been rather a lot, and they were continuing up until the day he was killed." Mantle shrugged his shoulders. "Perhaps he found it difficult to get rid of them."

Rick nodded. He agreed with Mantle's summing up of Deschamps from what he had learned of him, and from the little that he knew of Anne, he agreed with Mantle's opinion of the marriage. But you can't run other people's lives for them. They have to make or mar their own. As he was thinking that, Mantle went on, "When I saw Anne was set on it, I gave my consent. People have to live their own lives."

"Uhuh. How long were you in the study last night?"

"Perhaps fifteen minutes. I couldn't be sure."

"You had not been in Fareham's bedroom first?"

"No. I had been going to lie down on the bed there, and then I thought I'd be much less likely to be noticed in the study and it was nearer."

"Where did you go last night when you went out again after taking Anne home?"

If Mantle was surprised by the question, he didn't show it. His face remained impassive. "To see a man."

"The police will need his name and address," said Rick.

"Every large firm such as mine has various contacts——" Mantle broke off. "How I dislike the American use of that word, but it is useful. One does not advertise one's contacts."

"To insure you justice," said Rick, remembering the dinner-table conversation.

"I don't suppose you have any illusions about big business," remarked Mantle. "I understand you've worked for oil companies."

"I haven't," admitted Rick, and went on, "How did you know that Deschamps was continuing with 'his women,' as you called it, up till yesterday?"

"Those things can't be hidden in a place like this."

"So it was you who were having him followed."

Mantle didn't deny it. "Anne means a lot to me, and I'm the only family she has. Elaine, her mother, was a very beautiful woman. Men used to stop in the street and stare after her. And she was good. She married my brother, Hugh. Hugh was a good deal like Deschamps. All the women ran after him. He had a lot of what is nowadays called 'charm.' And he was always going off and doing some harum-scarum thing.

"He made Elaine's life a hell. There was never any money. Good-time Charley couldn't be bothered settling down to make a living or paying his debts when he did make something. He was always full of wonderful ideas about something that was going to make a great fortune. Some of his ideas weren't bad, but he'd never put any hard work behind them or he got tired of them. Women helped him and made their husbands help him. There was a series of them. It stopped for a few months when he married, but after about a year he never came home at night.

"Elaine never complained. I watched her age twenty years in ten. She was proud. She'd rather scrub floors than take help. I went down on my bended knees to her, begged her to let me help them, if not for her sake, for Anne's. But she wouldn't. But she used to say, 'Howard, if anything happens to me, you'll look after Anne, won't you?' As if she had a premonition.

"Finally she let me pay Anne's schooling. Things were going from bad to worse with Hugh, and she wanted Anne away. It nearly broke her heart, sending her to Switzerland, but she did it for the child's sake. When they were killed in the train wreck, I was left guardian for Anne. And I saw her starting to do just what her mother did before her. But I didn't intend her to go into it blindly. D'you understand?"

"So you had him watched."

"Exactly."

"Anne's very like her mother, isn't she?"

"Sometimes when she comes into a room, I——" Mantle stopped and got up. "I suppose you're going to this play tonight. Oh yes, you said you were."

"D'you think the drama is going to be on stage or out front?"

Mantle smiled sourly. "You'll have all your cast of the murder present, I expect."

As soon as he'd gone, Rick went out, took Sales's car, and drove to the home address of M. Mars. When he explained himself, the little Frenchman welcomed him hospitably in the small apartment on Junin, introduced his wife, brought out a bottle of sherry, and looked expectant.

"You've recently been digging out the record of the Downs murder case," said Rick. "Why?"

"M. Deschamps asked me to."

"When?"

"Five or six weeks ago. I employed a relation of my wife's to do the work as I hadn't time."

"So you did more than just dig out the police and newspaper records."

"Esteban, that is my wife's cousin, interviewed the one surviving parent of the girl who committed suicide and the son of the porter. Also one of the clerks who worked at that time in the office and is now working for the YPF."

"And what did you get?"

Mars shrugged. "Nothing that had not come out in the newspaper and police reports. Whatever the porter knew, he had not told his son. The son was quite small when his father died. Not more than ten. He said he remembered his mother talking about it occasionally, but he didn't think that she knew anything."

"Did Deschamps give you any reason for wanting the material?"

"He did not say, but as we knew that he hoped to marry Mlle. Mantle it seemed reasonable that he should want to know something about her family."

"How long did it take Esteban to do all this?"

"A week. No, it was ten days. There was a strike of transportation which delayed him."

"So about a month ago Deschamps had the information."

"Yes."

"And three weeks ago the announcement of his marriage was made," said Rick, half to himself. "Mantle had withdrawn his objections."

M. Mars looked up. "But everyone knows the story."

"Not quite everyone," said Rick. "That's the trouble."

CHAPTER 10

Stephen Sales was depressed when Rick picked him up. "If only one could do something instead of sitting waiting for something to happen. I think Fresne has the right idea."

"Which is what?"

"He's doing a spot of investigating on his own, he says."

"That'll be a lot of help," said Rick grimly.

"No use for amateurs?"

"They usually get underfoot. What's made him constitute himself detective?"

"He argues if Elting was killed because he knew something about the killing of Deschamps, because he, Fresne, and Dorothy Vidal were talking to Elting afterward, the murderer may decide they have the same information. He says anything is better than suspense. He came into my office today and practically took up the rug and looked in the wastebasket before he'd sit down, and then he put his back to a wall. He's got it badly."

"Wonder if he does know anything."

"He says he doesn't, but he isn't sure the murderer knows it."

"And assuming you to be the murderer, he thought he'd come and tell you?"

"Might have been."

"I'll find out if he's made the rounds of all the possibilities," said Rick. "He must have had quite a busy day."

The small theater where the performance was to be given was contained inside a large office building. As seems to be inevitable with amateur performances, more of the audience seemed to be backstage than out front, and those who were in front were all standing in groups talking, so that the ushers were becoming increasingly confused about the seating arrangements.

People stared at Steve, and several times the conversation among a group which they were passing died down abruptly, to the accompaniment of warning glances. Once Rick heard a high-pitched voice saying, "Of all the nerve! To come here!"

Steve had a seat near the Farehams. "We can do something about getting Mr. Vanner a seat—can't we, Bob?" said Louise. "I'm going to call you Rick, may I?"

"Please. But don't bother about the seat. I want to drift around." As he made his way backstage, Rick noticed the *subjefe*, Señor Boggia, talking to several men in plain clothes. On the stage itself, all was confusion. Fragments of speech reached him. "—a small box with the sewing kit." "It must be here. I saw it when I unpacked the tea things." "No flowers till the end. There's no room for them back here." "Anne's here and ready. I've told everybody to be very quiet and careful." "It worked at the dress rehearsal."

That was in an exasperated male voice. "He says the switch won't carry the load." "Why not? It did on Sunday." "Something about the police insisting the lights must be on in the outside passage when the hall is full."

It all seemed the normal confusion attendant on amateur theatricals. Dozens of people hurrying back and forth in a small space, getting in each other's way, all appearing frightfully busy.

"Throw it now, Mrs. Rockwell," called a voice from behind the set.

A dumpy woman with a string to which a weight was attached proceeded to swing it round her head in the manner of a lasso, endangering everyone around her. She finally threw, nearly knocked herself over with the effort, and the weight merely slapped against the wall of the set. As she prepared to try again, Rick took it from her. "Where d'you want it?"

"The weight's got to go over the other side. It holds up this picture," said Mrs. Rockwell. He threw it and heard a voice from the other side say, "Got it." Mrs. Rockwell was beaming ecstatically. "That's wonderful! I don't know you, do I? Next time we have a production, you must help."

Another voice was saying, "We've got to have the green spotlight and the cable simply isn't long enough."

"There's a man here who's simply wonderful," screamed Mrs. Rockwell. "Do come and see if you can help." She towed Rick by the hand to where two men were sadly surveying the green spotlight and an extension cable which would not reach to the only available plug.

"Why don't you use this piece?" asked Rick, pointing to a coil of some three feet of cable on the floor.

"There are no plugs for it," said one of the men.

"If you've got a pliers I can fix it for you."

"There should be pliers, but——" said the other man dubiously, and disappeared.

"Can you really fix it? I mean without blowing everything to hell?" asked the first man.

Rick took the plug on the end of the spotlight cable and started to dismantle it with his pocketknife.

"Aren't you wonderful!" Mrs. Rockwell screamed again. "Knowing how to do these things. Have you been in the theater?"

"No, ma'am. The navy," he told her.

Her attention was claimed elsewhere. The man, relieved to have found someone who understood the elements of electricity, drifted off. People were still dashing round looking for lost or forgotten articles. A voice kept saying, "Have you a needle and thread?"

"Mr. Vanner——" Rick looked up and saw Anne beside him, dressed in a maid's uniform, her blond hair scraped into a bun on the top of her head.

"All ready, I see."

"If I sit in the dressing room one minute longer, I'll do something frightful. They all whisper when I'm around, as if someone were very ill or they were in church or something. Why can't they behave naturally?"

"People do that," said Rick. "Hang onto this, will you?"

"How did you get pressed into service?"

"Nobody seemed to have seen an electric cable before, and self-defense being the first law of nature, I volunteered."

"I don't see the connection."

"I was uncomfortably close if there was going to be an explosion."

"You are a fool!"

"I know, but don't tell anyone. Hold this one too."

"They won't——" She looked a bit dubiously at the cables.

"No, they won't. One of the nice things about electric current is that there isn't any when they aren't hooked up."

"I *know* that." A minute later she said, "I hated leaving Justine alone in the house. She looked so ill and worn."

"She is tired," agreed Rick carelessly.

"I know. She came down to dinner but she hardly ate anything."

"Now." He took one of the lines from her. "I suppose it would be too much to expect them to find even such a rudimentary tool as a pliers around here?"

"There probably are, but nobody would know where."

"I thought so." He continued working. "Or insulating material, either. I shall have to sacrifice a handkerchief in the cause of the drama."

"Why?"

"Any insulation is better than none."

"Yes. Mr. Vanner——"

"What is it?"

"Have you seen—I mean is——"

"Steve has not been arrested and was in quite reasonably good health when I left him out front about ten minutes ago."

"Oh. I wanted to know."

"Oh. You're the electrician!" Another fat little woman

rushed up. "Thank goodness you've got here. The turn-table's got to be fixed."

"But, Mrs. Strawbridge, this is Mr. Vanner," protested Anne.

"Never mind his name, dear, now that he's here."

"Your turntable can't go on this, as there seems to be a complete absence of three-way plugs," Rick told her.

"Oh dear. I wonder if——" She rushed off.

Anne shook her head. "She can get in more people's way than any other three women. But she means awfully well."

"The most damning remark you can make about a human being. Now—if that man who is going to work this would appear . . ."

"Who was he?"

"No idea. He looked like a rabbit crossed with a lobster. The facial contours were that of a rabbit. The color, as in a well-boiled lobster." Rick looked hopefully round.

With unflattering promptitude, Anne said, "That's Ted Wrighton. Ted—where's Ted? His lamp's all fixed."

"I say, you haven't really fixed it, have you?" Mr. Wrighton had reached the point where if anything went right he didn't believe it.

"It's okay for tonight," said Rick. "But don't handle it roughly. It isn't properly insulated and might be danger-ous."

"You think if I throw the switch now it'll be okay?" Ted Wrighton did not sound quite convinced.

Rick looked over at the board, found the number, reached across and threw the switch. A baleful green light flooded the vicinity.

"My God, you're a genius! All the electrical stuff here

147

is so old that the professional electrician refused to come again after our last show."

"I can quite believe it," said Rick dryly.

"Please will all the visitors leave the stage," a voice was pleading.

Like a refrain came, "Has anybody got a needle and thread?"

Rick grinned at Anne. "Seems to me it would be much less trouble just to send a check to the charity."

"*Please* clear stage. Curtain is going up in two minutes." The voice sounded on the verge of tears.

"I'd better go before I'm thrown."

"You're awfully kind and you do understand things," said Anne. "Thanks a lot."

As he crossed to go back into the hall he passed Gloria, made up with gray grease paint as the ghost wife. She said, "I don't go on till half through the act and I'm getting more nervous every minute. Did Douglas and Mother get here?"

"I didn't see them, but I've been backstage the last ten or fifteen minutes."

"Are you—no, don't tell me anything. I've a horrible feeling something is going to happen."

Rick went along the passage outside the auditorium and met the *subjefe,* who said, "Ah, Señor Vanner, you are interested in the drama?"

"The on-stage one or the other?" asked Rick.

Boggia smiled a bit wanly. "The French Embassy wants to know why no one has been arrested. My chief wants to know why no one has been arrested. The British newspaper wants to know why no one has been arrested. A murder case would be so enjoyable if it were not for outside pressure."

Having never classified murder cases under the heading of diversions, Rick was silent for a moment. "May I ask how many men you've got here tonight?"

"Twenty. Ten plain-clothes and ten uniformed."

"Expecting trouble or just playing safe?"

"Everyone seemed very nervous."

"Michel Fresne—or everyone?"

"Ah. He has talked to you also, señor."

"He has talked to everyone," said Rick. "I have a favor to ask you. If you would use your discretion about reporting something officially."

"If I can, señor." Boggia was curious.

Briefly Rick explained about the attempt on Justine. "I questioned her and the chauffeur and that is all they can tell me."

"You think if it is not mentioned, the murderer will find himself confused," said Boggia hopefully.

"He might."

"But supposing he tries again?"

"She's safe enough in Mantle's house," said Rick.

"Very well. If you think it is advisable not to mention it, I will do as you ask. And I wanted to consult you. The *comisario* and I have a plan for tomorrow evening. I am asking all the people concerned to come to the Fareham apartment at seven o'clock."

"And then reconstruct the crime or what?"

"Oh no, señor. I enjoy the Hollywood *cines*, but I do not learn my business from them. I want to recapitulate where everybody sat and stood and what they talked about from the time when they rose from the table to the time when the body was found. There are still gaps. I think that, with them all together, what one forgets another may remember."

"May be interesting," said Rick. "Any news on the gun that killed Elting?"

"None. But more important than the gun is, how did the murderer get in? None of the tenants admits letting anyone in last night. And think of the risk. In the first place, he did not know when Elting would return. And perhaps no tenant would have let him in before. Unless he entered before the doors were locked at nine o'clock and remained hidden."

"Making it someone who was not at the dinner and therefore not connected with the Deschamps killing," said Rick, and added, "Had you thought the murderer might have returned with Elting and walked in with him?"

The *subjefe* was still looking surprised as Rick drifted into the auditorium. It was not a very good performance, although Noel Coward's play is almost foolproof or actorproof as a laugh-getter. Finally the curtain fell on the first act. Rick's eyes roamed over the audience. Douglas Canning and Gloria's mother were quite near where he was standing. Gloria, with her gray make-up, was signaling from the pass door, trying to get her husband or her mother's attention. Several delivery boys with flowers were arguing with police.

Michel Fresne and a man were talking near Rick. "Spunky of Anne Mantle to go through with her part."

"She is courageous," agreed Fresne.

Douglas Canning had gone up to the pass door.

"Matter of fact," Fresne's companion was continuing, "come to think of it, it's more spunky of Gloria. That affair——"

The little old lady was less than three feet away. Rick moved forward. He said, quite flatly, "Come here."

The surprised gossiper found his arm taken and before he knew it he was being propelled toward the main exit. He spluttered, as if his mouth was full of hot plums, "Who'-th'hell d'you think you are?"

"The name's Vanner."

"Take your hands off me."

Fresne had followed, saying rather vaguely, "He's the detective."

"Just be careful how you bandy people's names round here," said Rick thinly. "Now you can go."

"Gloria got you on the string too?" The man gave an unpleasant laugh.

"Mrs. Canning's mother was two seats away from you."

"Oh my God!" said the man, forgetting his temper in his agitation. "Did she hear?"

"I hope not." Rick turned on his heel. Fresne followed him.

"Who was in that taxi today?"

"Some little punk," said Vanner carelessly.

"But what did you say or do?"

"He didn't follow you any more, did he? So what are you worrying about?"

Fresne was watching him shrewdly. "It is not a comfortable feeling that there is a murderer in a group with which one is so closely associated. *Mon Dieu!* I find myself looking for walls to put my back against." He repeated his anxiety over what the murderer might have thought Elting had told him and Dorothy Vidal. "I told the police I felt that Mme. Vidal should have an escort."

Rick was watching Fresne's thin face as he played with the upper lip. He was a bad color and looked as if he hadn't slept.

"When you were in Fareham's bathroom last night, was the door tried?"

Fresne's eyes were calculating. "Yes. Yes. I think it was."

The second act was starting. There were considerably fewer contretemps and everybody seemed to be getting into his stride. The curtain came down to a satisfactory amount of applause.

Dorothy Vidal was en route out to the lobby to smoke. She left her two escorts and came to Rick.

"Murder cases don't get cleared up in half a day," he told her in answer to her question as to how it was progressing.

"What d'you think of the show? Of course poor Gloria's so upset. But she's doing wonderfully, considering——"

"I thought she was very good. And she doesn't seem a bit upset," said Rick irritatingly.

A wave of annoyance crossed her face. "Have you asked Douglas Canning why he stuffed Gloria's gloves in his pocket in such a hurry?" She turned to call to her escort, "Yes, I'm coming."

"One more thing, Mme. Vidal. Where were you when you saw Mantle in the passage last night?"

"Just coming out of Louise's bedroom."

"He didn't see you."

"Of course not. He had his back to me. Yes, darling, I'm coming." The last half was to the escort.

Rick watched Fresne follow her as he hurried out to the lobby. There was a distinct annoyance on the Frenchman's face. Finally the third act got under way—and finished. The curtain came down, flowers were passed up, speeches were made, and friends swarmed backstage. Rick found Steve Sales.

"There's a supper, you know. I'm not going. I've had all I can take of sideways glances and whispering behind my back. I'm liable to smack someone down any minute."

"It's the Plaza, isn't it? I may look in on my way upstairs."

"Want the car? The Farehams will drop me if you do."

"Thanks. Yes, I may. What do I do about getting gas?"

Sales explained the complicated system by which one gets gasoline in Buenos Aires.

A good deal of the audience and nearly all the people he had seen backstage were at the supper party, which was showing a quite remarkable gaiety. A variety of people he hardly knew came up to Vanner and propounded theories about the killing, including one loud-voiced, horse-faced female who was sure they were the work of the Cannings' chauffeur. When asked on what she based her theory, she announced, "He's a bad-mannered lout and speaks French."

"Has anyone told you," inquired a pimply-faced woman with a snub nose, "that Dot Vidal's husband died in most *peculiar* circumstances, from ptomaine poisoning? At least, they *said* it was ptomaine after a party where *nobody* else got ill, and *she* was there."

Rick looked over at the widow, who was surrounded, as usual, by a group of men. "She is pretty, isn't she?"

"Oh. *Do* you think so?" Snub Nose stared. "Anyway, what's that got to do with it?"

"Hasn't it?" inquired Rick maliciously. He heard Bob Fareham's voice near him, speaking to Louise.

"You're not enjoying yourself one scrap, my dear, so let's go home. We've put in our appearance."

Rick turned and said, "I've got to pester you with some questions soon."

"Come up to the house and do it in comfort," said Louise. "This zoo is giving me a pain."

"Me too," agreed Rick.

CHAPTER 11

They walked in silence down the short piece of sidewalk between the Plaza Hotel and the Kavanaugh Building. When they finally reached the apartment, Louise threw her tiny hat onto one chair, her coat onto another, and herself onto the sofa. For a second she lay back, reveling in the luxury of getting home. Then she gave an apprehensive glance in the direction of the arch that led to the dining room and to the other arch that led to the passage and bedrooms. Bob had put on only the living-room light. He was now standing by the bar.

"Like us to give the place the once-over?" asked Rick, interpreting her glance.

She smiled up at him. "If I were twenty years younger and not married to Bob, I'd fall in love with you. Thank you. I'll make no bones about it. I'd feel much happier if you'd go over the house."

"Let the poor man have his drink, Louise," protested her husband. "As soon as I've got the ice, I'll take a look round."

But Rick had already switched on the passage light. He went rapidly into the study, opened the one cupboard, was nearly gassed by the moth balls inside, and closed it hurriedly. Louise's bedroom and bathroom revealed no intruder. He snapped up the light in Bob's bedroom, went into the bathroom, and then stood in the passage doorway for some time.

"Are you all right?" came Louise's voice.

"Of course he's all right," answered Bob. "Probably went to the——"

Rick came back to the living room. "I've even looked under the beds," he reported. "But remind me to bring a gas mask next time I'm going to open your cupboards."

"That must have been the one in the study. I should have warned you. Though I suppose someone could hide in it."

"Not for long," said Rick.

"Louise isn't prone to jitters," said Bob. "You take water with it, don't you? I've given you water."

"Thanks." Rick took a drink. "Glad you told me."

"What?"

"That there is water."

"Want more?"

"No, thanks. Water is stuff to go under bridges."

"I can't help being jittery," said Louise.

"Don't blame you," said Rick. "Murder is a nasty thing."

"You know, during the war—the first World War—I got fairly used to corpses around. I never liked 'em, but I don't think they bothered me much, after a while." Bob looked at his drink. "But I can't say I like murder in my house."

"It's the feeling that he's still around. The murderer."

Louise was practical. "Even if he'd shot him decently from in front, it wouldn't be so bad."

"Also, there's no denying it's a damned uncomfortable feeling looking at people and wondering if they did it," went on Bob. "And knowing they're looking at us in the same way. It happened in our house."

"D'you suppose they think that?" demanded Louise. "But why?"

"We were here," said her husband.

"But why on earth should we kill him? We liked him enough to ask him to dinner. Why, we'd often had him here to the house."

"Luring him to his doom."

"But seriously, Bob, there are an awful lot of people I don't like enough to ask them to the house and I still don't dislike them enough to want to kill them. I just avoid meeting people I dislike. The world's large enough."

"I've been told today that everybody, including you, Vanner, probably was the murderer, which means that our dear good friends all suspect each other and, it follows, us."

"What was my motive?" asked Rick. "Or did they just take me for a homicidal maniac?"

"It was very complicated," Fareham explained. "And based on the idea that you weren't what you represented yourself to be. You had probably killed the real Richard Vanner and were masquerading as him with a view to killing Deschamps."

"Somebody has been reading the more lurid pulps," said Rick. "Why should this person who killed Vanner want to kill Deschamps?"

"God knows. We didn't get as far as that. I was explaining that we really knew who you were when, thank God, my secretary came in and said someone was waiting."

"Who was responsible for this notion?"

"Tom Winthrop."

"A would-be mastermind," said Louise. "Just married and lives downstairs in the Linari apartment while they're away. Used to write short stories and now works for an advertising firm."

"Need a fiction talent to write copy," said Bob. "Matter of fact, the fellow only ever wrote a couple of things which were never published."

"Can you remember who talked to Deschamps last night, before dinner?" Rick brought them back to business a few minutes later.

"I was so busy with the drinks," said Bob.

"How about you?" Rick looked at Louise.

"People circulated pretty well. It wasn't one of those dreadfully static things where everybody gets glued to a chair and never moves," said Louise.

"Try to remember everything you did and saw from when he arrived to when dinner was served."

"Have another whisky, Louise," suggested Bob.

She had another. "Well, he and Justine and Steve all arrived together. I took Justine in to leave her coat."

"I'd just fixed Anne's drink when they came," put in Bob. "Mantle and I were talking about Miranda's speech."

"Dot Vidal came next, and I introduced her to Justine and she asked her how she liked B.A. and the poor woman said, 'I only arrived yesterday,' and right on top Arrietti arrived and asked her the same thing."

"Dot wanted some extraordinary mixture to drink," put

in Bob. "She never can settle for anything other people are having."

"What happened next?" Louise stared at the ceiling. "Oh, Michel Fresne arrived and I wondered if he was going to greet the unfortunate Justine with 'What do you think of B.A.?' I told Steve I was ready to bet."

"Did he?" asked Rick.

"No. He was so surprised, he didn't."

"Surprised?"

"Well, he wasn't, but we were."

"Why?"

"I introduced him to Justine, and then Henri said, 'M. Fresne, have we ever met?' And it had never occurred to me that they wouldn't have met. You know what a small French colony it is here. So we were all being surprised and saying how odd it was, and Justine escaped without being asked. But sure enough Fred Elting arrived a couple of minutes later and he said it.

"People got sorted out. I noticed Fresne and Elting round Dot like flies round a honeypot. Mantle and Henri were having some discussion over there——" Louise pointed to the corner near the dining room.

"Then the Cannings arrived, and Gloria and I went into the bedroom and we were talking about her mother and if she'd like to come for lunch or tea. And she fiddled around for ages, fixing her face and her hair, and I thought she didn't want to come in and face Henri. She's been running around with him a lot, you know, before his engagement was announced. Anyway, we finally came in, and she asked Justine what she thought of B.A.

"That made everybody except you, and I knew you'd be

late. Elting and Henri were having a discussion about the wisdom or otherwise of France having devalued the franc when she did or whatever it was. I didn't listen. I just heard enough to know it was something like that, and then Steve got in the argument. And a bit later Arrietti took Henri off into the passage and talked to him. Henri looked upset when he came back, I thought, and went to Anne.

"I didn't notice him for a while. I remember Fred was talking about the fight and I was trying to be intelligent about it and remember what Bob had said so I could sound as if I had once seen a prize fight. I haven't.

"Then somebody knocked over that little table over there and a bowl of olives flew all over the floor. And I went to see if any damage was done. You know, if anyone's dress had got messed, but thank God it hadn't. And we all fielded olives. And after that . . . let's see. I got talking to Michel Fresne about St. Malo and——"

"How did that come up?" interrupted Rick.

"Bob and I spent our honeymoon there."

"But what started the discussion on it?"

"Somebody must have said something——" Louise stopped.

"Make a wonderful witness, my wife," grinned Bob. "D'you think a hushed and reverent quiet will help her most or another scotch?"

"Shut up. I'm thinking." Louise made a face at him.

"The only contribution I can make," said Bob, "while Louise is engaged in this profound thought, is that I heard Anne tick off Gloria about France during the war."

"What did she say?"

"I imagine Gloria must have said the French didn't put

up a good show or something like that, because Anne said, 'I don't think those of us who didn't have an occupying army on top of us have any right to judge them.' "

"I know," said Louise suddenly. "Henri was talking to Michel. I didn't hear what they were saying. But he said St. Malo, something or another, 1943—and I said, 'St. Malo, d'you know it? Bob and I spent our honeymoon there.' It wasn't a terribly bright remark, but it made something to say. And Henri said, 'My recollections of St. Malo are not so pleasant.'

"And Michel gave me a light because I was waving a cigarette. I don't really smoke, except at times like those. Cocktail parties and women's lunches. It gives me something to fidget with. And Anne came up and said something to Henri. Asked what he'd done to make her uncle cross."

"What did she say? D'you remember?"

" 'Have you been having a row with Uncle?' or something like that, and Henri said, 'No, a difference of opinion,' and Fred Elting made a crack about that being the diplomatic way of putting it." Louise broke off and said, "It does give one a queer feeling now that both of them are dead." She ran on without a pause. "I do feel I should have insisted more with Justine that she stay here last night. But I felt she wanted to be alone. She's gone to the Mantles' now, I hear."

"I think she's only done that to make Anne feel better," said Rick.

"That woman," said Bob slowly, looking at his drink, "has that kind of zero-hour courage that faces things without any attempt at escape."

It was such a shrewd remark coming from the bumbling, good-natured Bob that it made Rick look up in surprise.

"It's a bitter kind of courage," he said, half to himself.

Louise put down her glass. "She's an oddly tragic figure, but one can't be sorry for her. Pity would be impertinent, if you know what I mean."

"I know exactly," said Rick. "You've been a big help. Thanks and good night."

When he returned to the Plaza, Rick received two messages. One, that the *subjefe* had called; second, that Dr. Arrietti was looking for him. He went in search of the doctor and found the supper party in full swing still, but with a queer atmosphere of unease hanging over it.

A dozen people spoke to him at once. He heard, "Disgraceful, I call it," and, "Dreadful at this hour of night," without being able to discover what was disgraceful or dreadful.

Finally he found Dr. Arrietti, who told him. "Gloria was picked up by the police and taken to the Central for questioning. Douglas went with her, of course. He wanted you told."

"Where are they? At the Central in Calle Moreno?"

"Yes."

"I'll go and see what's happening," Rick promised.

At the Central the *subjefe* was courteous. "I tried to reach you. All day my men have been questioning the three extra maids employed last night by the Farehams. One of them had told the others that she knew who did it. Finally she has broken down. She says she saw the Señora Canning coming from Señor Fareham's bedroom. She looked round to be sure that she was not observed." The *subjefe* beamed.

"We know that the Señora Canning had been conducting an illicit affair with Deschamps. He announces his marriage. Mad with jealousy, she kills him."

"Hm. How did she kill Elting?"

"We may have been mistaken in thinking that these two murders are linked," said Boggia. "We have further proof against the Señora Canning. Her gloves have disappeared. We have been told they were bloodstained. Her husband says he lost them. Another thing," he added craftily, "if it were not the Señora Canning, perhaps her husband, infuriated with the knowledge of her unfaithfulness——"

"Where's the maid?" asked Rick.

The maid looked tired and frightened. Her name was Demetria. "Just tell me what you've told the police," said Rick.

"I was bringing more ice. As I came through the door from the kitchen to the passage I stopped and I saw the señora by the señor's bedroom door. She did not see me, because I had stopped in the doorway to change the tray from one hand to the other so that I could close the door. And she looked up and down the passage and then went and joined the others."

"You're very observant," Rick complimented her. "What was she wearing?"

"She had on her blue sequin dress. The señor saw it."

"Did she have her wrap?"

"No."

"What was she carrying?"

"A gold sequin bag."

"Did she have her gloves on?"

"No."

Rick looked at Boggia, who said, "If she'd found she had made them bloody, she'd obviously have taken them off."

"Obviously. But equally obviously, she wouldn't have left them lying around."

Boggia looked a bit disconcerted. "She might just have wanted to get rid of them. Hoped they would become lost."

Vanner put his head on one side. "And so she left them in full view on the end table?"

"Perhaps she had not noticed that they were bloody." The *subjefe* brightened up again. "She would take them off as soon as she had done the deed, not requiring them any more as a guard against leaving fingerprints. In the emotion of the moment, she does not see that they are bloody and puts them down on the table." He was quite dramatic. "Anyway, why was she coming out of Fareham's bedroom?"

"The maid said she was by the door. She had to pass the door anyway, coming from Louise's room."

A subordinate came in and said. "The Señor Canning wants to talk to you, Señor Boggia."

"Now perhaps we'll learn something. I have kept them separate."

"I'd like to speak to Canning for a moment."

Boggia expressed himself as delighted and bowed Vanner out ahead of him. They went into a small room where Douglas Canning was seated at a table. An ash tray beside him held a pile of half-smoked cigarettes. He looked ill and deadly tired.

"Vanner, what are they doing to Gloria?" he demanded.

"Relax," Rick told him. "They won't beat her up." His eyes flicked over the two *agentes* in the room. A signal had passed between Boggia and one of them. With a shrewd idea that the man spoke, or at least understood, English, Rick picked his words carefully. "D'you remember what I told you in my room?"

"What?" Canning frowned as if he momentarily felt the remark irrelevant.

"That this investigation was going on until we got the truth, regardless of what it was." Rick's gray eyes were fixed on him with a compelling hardness. "So don't do anything stupid. It won't help anyone. Understand?"

"But Gloria——"

"Is perfectly all right."

"They think she——"

"They can't prove it."

For a moment Canning looked straight at Rick, and the pain in his eyes made the detective wince. He wondered what that pain might drive him to do, or might have driven him to do.

"*Señor subjefe*"—Rick turned to Boggia—"I wonder if it wouldn't give better results to let these people go until tomorrow. Today, rather. Perhaps your plan will work better than this individual questioning."

Boggia looked shrewdly at him. "I did not think that you approved much of my plan."

"I have been thinking about it since. I feel you have assessed the temperament of this group of people better than I. Together in a bunch, you'll find it easier to discover who is lying . . ." Rick went on for some time. Finally it worked.

The Cannings were released. Gloria's face, which showed streaks of tears on the make-up, was drawn and tired. She

165

came to Rick and whispered, "They know—and Mother——"

He shook his head. "They won't talk."

He watched them go out and shook his head. It didn't seem to occur to her that her husband might be hurt by knowing of her affair if he did not already know. Or if it did occur to her, she didn't seem to mind. He turned back to Señor Boggia.

"I was going to call you in the morning and ask what you thought of putting men on all the cafés or places with telephones that are open all night within a reasonable radius of Elting's Esmeralda apartment and all the night places en route between Olivos and the Centro. Find out if they remember anyone stopping in between three and six to telephone, and get a description."

Boggia looked in the direction in which the Cannings had gone. "Olivos," he muttered. "It is an excellent idea."

When he finally did get to bed, Rick took the lists he had made the night before and again considered the time schedule. The late Fred Elting had been to and returned from the bedroom sufficiently long before the killing not to have seen the murderer in the passage and had remained leaning against the radio until after the body had been discovered. If he had been killed because of something he knew, it was not because of something he had seen on his trip to the bathroom. His position by the radio, though, had been an excellent one for noticing if anyone took the poncho pin.

Why did nobody remember noticing Deschamps from about five minutes after they came out from dinner until his body was found? Where had he been? There were, at any rate, two women in the room who should have known.

Women in love do know when the man they love is present.

It was not a large apartment. There had been someone in Louise's room at all times. There had been people in Bob's room. The maids reported that no one had come out to the kitchen. The maids also reported that no one had come into the dining room where they were clearing away. Deschamps might have ridden down in the elevator to the lobby, but there seemed no reason why he should have done.

He might have gone into the study. The telephone, which was of the kind that could be plugged into different rooms, had been in there. He might have wanted to phone. But he had left there before Mantle went in, because Mantle hadn't seen him. Of course Mantle wasn't too sure of the time when he had gone into the study, which was not surprising in view of his heart condition.

Vanner racked his own photographic memory and checked the stories against it. He hadn't been attending and he had been in a corner, but he was prepared to swear that Deschamps had not been in the living room for a good ten minutes before his body was found. He finally put out the light, still pondering on the remarkable fact of the late Henri Deschamps' invisibility.

CHAPTER 12

Seminario rang up early with information about the two
addresses Rick had found at the French Embassy. "I sent
a man last night. Good time to catch those sort of people.
You were quite right. They were the home addresses of
two maids who'd worked for Vidal. They've both got other
jobs now."

"D'you know where?"

The detective furnished him with addresses. "None of
your people did anything interesting in the afternoon or
evening of yesterday," Seminario went on, "except Michel
Fresne, who had what my man called a 'suspicious'-looking
visitor waiting for him when he got home last night, very
late. Two-thirty. He went up to Fresne's apartment with
him and remained about half an hour."

"Your man didn't follow him?"

"No. Instructions were to cover Fresne."

"Damn——"

"I'm having the reports typed up," said Seminario.

Of the two maids' addresses, one was in Belgrano and the other in the center. Rick decided to do the Belgrano one first and then come back into the center, leave Sales's car somewhere safe, and use taxis. After his parking experiences of the day before, he had decided that a car in the town was a liability rather than an asset.

The house where Sofia Collado worked was an opulent-looking place of an architectural atrociousness unequaled in Vanner's experience. He went to the back door, which was opened by an enormously fat woman, who turned round and called, "Sofia—a señor asking for you." She turned back, looked him over again, apparently approved, and invited him into the kitchen. A girl of about twenty-five appeared, hurriedly patting her hair into place. Rick explained his mission.

"I remember the señor who came a few weeks ago. He asked a lot of questions, but he did not tell me why."

The cook brought a small cup of coffee and gave it to Rick, putting in two lumps of sugar before he could stop her.

"What were the questions?"

"He wanted to know about the Señora Vidal. I was working for her in 1944. It was my first job. I got it through my mother's brother-in-law, who was the porter. Señora Vidal lived at Juncal—then. This señor also wanted to know if I could tell him anything about a Señor Fremont who came to visit." She gave a little giggle. "The Señor Fremont came when the Señor Vidal was out. The Señor Vidal traveled a lot, and when he was away the Señor Fremont used to come. At first I did not know what to think, but then I learned that those things are always done by rich people and foreigners.

"Señora Vidal used to have wonderful parties," she went on. "Here the señora doesn't give many, and only to her family. But Señora Vidal used to have all the diplomatic people. Sometimes very big parties, when the Señor Vidal was there, but when he was away, small ones."

"And Fremont was invited to them all?"

She nodded. "And he used to stay after everyone else was gone. She would say to me, 'Sofia, I shan't need anything else. You can go to bed.'"

"Did Fremont ever come when Vidal was there?"

"At first he used to. Later, he never did. They had a terrible quarrel one day. We heard them from the kitchen. But it was all in French and we couldn't understand."

"Why did you leave Señora Vidal?"

"When she moved from Juncal, after the señor died, she said she did not want anyone who had been there while he was alive. She said it reminded her." The girl shrugged her shoulders. "She paid us what was due."

"Did she ever talk about the war? About the Nazis?"

"She did not speak much Spanish. Just enough to say what she wanted done."

In due course Rick took his leave, thanked the cook for the coffee, and left a twenty-peso bill behind with Sofia.

The other maid's place of work on Parana was not so opulent. It was a rather drab apartment block, and Theresa was evidently the only servant in the apartment. She had just returned from the market and had her coat still on as she unpacked a bag of foodstuffs on the kitchen table.

"I remember him. He never did tell me why he was asking so many questions," she answered Rick, and eyed him suspiciously.

"Does it matter why?" Rick was folding a twenty-peso bill between his fingers.

Theresa looked at the bill. "No. I've no reason to be grateful to her anyway."

"What did she do to you?"

It seemed that the Señora Vidal had missed some money and accused Theresa of taking it. "I can defend myself. There were things that she didn't want talked about, she with her husband hardly dead in his grave. *And* dead of poisoning. So I left."

"And these things she didn't want talked about, what were they? The Señor Fremont?"

Rick got substantially the same story from her that he had heard from Sofia. The only difference was that Theresa flatly stated that Fremont had been Mme. Vidal's lover. He put the twenty-peso bill into the overwilling hand and left.

The office of Gaston Daume, with whom Michel Fresne had been in brief partnership, was on Corrientes. Mr. Daume was elderly and did not seem enthusiastic when Rick said he wanted to learn something about Fresne. "How did you meet him?"

Daume chewed the end of his untidy mustache. "A sum in Swiss francs was sent to me early in 1945 to keep for him," he said. "When Fresne arrived he was looking for an investment."

"Where did the money come from?"

Daume shrugged. "It was sent through a friend of mine in Switzerland."

"A German friend?"

171

"No, monsieur, a Swiss. Where it came from before my friend had it, I did not know or ask."

Rick didn't pursue the subject. "Why didn't you continue your business association with Fresne?"

"We did not agree."

"On what?"

"Business methods."

"Is he crooked?" asked Rick bluntly.

"If I hear that a factory is about to be built in a certain district, I will go and buy land there. If the factory needs my land, they must buy from me. Naturally I make a profit. That is business. But I do not go and buy worthless land and hire some hoodlums to go round the district telling lies and saying that a factory is going to be built, and then offer my worthless land for sale." M. Daume chewed his mustache vigorously.

"I see. What else?"

"What else!" He was dramatic. "I am a cautious man, monsieur, I did not wait to find out."

"But you're not so cautious that you don't help smuggle funds out of Europe."

"You must not forget, monsieur, that Switzerland was neutral."

"That's all I wanted to know."

Back at the Plaza, Rick found the usual batch of telephone messages. Wishing at the moment that the telephone had never been invented, he went up to his room and started to call the people. Douglas Canning was the first. Canning wanted to talk to him, but not on the phone.

"If you don't say any more than you did last night, you'll be wasting our time," retorted Rick. "I've several things to get done this afternoon. If I can, I'll call your office or stop in."

Gloria Canning, when he got her, also wanted to talk to him, but not on the phone. "I'm frantic," she said. "What is this meeting tonight? What's going to happen? What are they going to say? I must see you before it." He promised to try to meet her in the Plaza lounge at four.

Fareham was next on the list. He also wanted to know about the conference. "The *comisario* wouldn't say what he was going to do. He was polite but vague. If I didn't mind—so much more convenient than calling everyone to headquarters—so much depended on the layout of the apartment—and so on. Nothing concrete. Louise has just about given up. She's sure there's going to be another murder and is afraid someone will put arsenic in our drinks!" Fareham laughed but he did not seem happy about the whole idea. "Louise asked me to get hold of you and see if you knew what it was all about."

"I don't exactly. The *subjefe* thinks it will be a bit easier to get all the details out of the people in a bunch, and that in the same rooms some things that have been genuinely forgotten may come to light. Tell Louise not to worry."

"Serve the death's-head cocktail and wear your best find-the-murderer suit," said Fareham. "Can't say the prospect thrills me. However, see you then."

Rick called Mme. Vidal and asked if he might call to see her after lunch. "I think you could help me," he told her.

Anything she could do to help him, she announced, she would be only too happy. She had been going to the hairdresser, but she'd postpone it. "You know—this meeting or whatever it is at the Farehams' tonight . . ."

Rick went down to the bar and nearly collided with Michel Fresne. "I hoped I might see you here," said the little Frenchman, pulling at his upper lip. "I telephoned the police this morning and they seem to have made no progress at all. None!"

"Police work takes time and patience," said Rick.

"In the meantime the murderer is at large, free to strike again."

"Very silly of him if he did. He's made enough blunders already."

"Blunders! If he's made blunders, why don't you and the police catch him?"

"The *comisario* follows his own methods and won't be hurried."

"What does he intend doing? Making a dramatic arrest at the Farehams' house? It is of a stupidity amazing!"

"Other people have been making blunders too," said Rick. "It's not only the murderer."

"Other people?"

"Uhuh. Come and have a drink. You look as if you needed one." When he'd ordered drinks Rick said, "I don't think the *comisario* is planning a dramatic arrest. Just wants to check up on some details."

"These Argentines! They should see how the French police work."

"The Germans are pretty good at that too. I heard the other day that some German officer or other was over here to help train their police."

"What's that? A German officer here training the police?"

"So I heard. Probably just a rumor."

"It's disgraceful! Shouldn't be permitted. Who is he?" Fresne seemed disturbed.

"No idea. Maybe it'll do something toward the efficiency of the local police. Though," added Rick, "as far as this case is concerned, they've been doing pretty well." Fresne gave a snort of disgust which seemed to indicate disagreement. "What would you have done?"

But no very concrete suggestions were forthcoming. "It is, I admit, not so easy. For we all had opportunity. Even you and I, monsieur. Though why either of us should wish to kill a man we have never met before, I don't know."

"It isn't usual, but it happens sometimes," said Rick.

"When there is a maniac at large."

"Not always maniacs." A waiter interrupted to say that a chauffeur was inquiring for Señor Vanner upstairs. Rick paid for the drinks over Fresne's protest and went up to the street.

Domingo was standing on the sidewalk at the entrance to the bar, looking harassed and a bit disapproving. "The Señorita Anne wants to speak to the señor," he said.

The car was across the street, by the steps leading to the park. Anne's face, unnaturally white and strained, looked out. She motioned Vanner to get in and told Domingo to "Drive around."

"I've been phoning you all morning. I tried this as a last hope," she said.

"What's gone wrong?" he asked.

"I didn't know who to go to. You were so kind, yesterday and last night." She made an apologetic little gesture. "Tell me what's happened."

"Mrs. Raines came over this morning. She wanted the

175

check Uncle had promised her for the hospital. She was very sweet and apologized for coming, but she said they were making up their books or something for tax liability and the accountant wanted to get it into the bank by a certain date. I didn't understand and I don't think she did either——"

"You have to be a tax expert to understand these things," said Rick cheerfully. "We ordinary mortals can never hope to."

"I took her to the study. Uncle often leaves checks for household bills and charities on his desk. I thought I'd look there before calling him at the office and asking him to send a boy with it. I was looking down at the papers and I saw a typewritten sheet with Henri's name on it. And I looked. I suppose I shouldn't have, but——"

"What was it?"

"It was a report from a detective. Uncle was having a man follow him. What does it all mean?"

"Checking up on the man his niece is going to marry," said Rick casually.

"One doesn't have a man followed, and you know it. Perhaps if it is someone you don't know anything about, you make a few inquiries, about their family and so on. But that's all."

"What was the report like?"

"I—I only looked at the front page."

He knew she was lying but he didn't say so. "Is that all that's bothering you?"

"No. I called Steve," she went on with forlorn irrelevance, "and he wouldn't meet me. He said we'd be sure to be seen and that it wouldn't do, for my sake, until the whole thing was cleared up. He told me to see you. He said if I asked you—I mean he said I could tell you things and you wouldn't talk."

"Go on. Tell me."

"I want you to do something to help me, and please don't ask me why."

"I can't make blind promises."

She thought for a moment and then said, "At one-thirty I am going to meet a man to pay him some money. I want to try to get some security that he will do what he has promised to do. I can't explain."

"Paying blackmail is a mug's game, Anne," he told her.

"I know all about that. But in this case it's the only way. Please believe me. I know."

"If it's silence you're buying," he said with an intentional brutality, "there is only one way to insure it. Kill the man with the information as soon as you're sure that only he possesses it."

She stared at him for a moment, then shook her head. "But it would be to his own advantage to keep his word."

"So that he can blackmail you again? Certainly. You'll have no security and you'll go on paying until you die or he does."

"But if you find the murderer, there'll be no reason," she began, and stopped.

Rick looked at his watch. Five to one. "Where d'you have to meet this man?"

"At that bar at the corner of Lavalle and Maipu."

"Turn back toward town and go slowly down the Avenida Alvear," he told Domingo. "Now listen, Anne, tell me what this is all about and I'll try and help you. I know a

177

great deal more about dealing with crooks and blackmailers —and about murder cases—than you do. But I can't help unless you give me the facts."

"I can't explain."

"Once the murderer is found, there'll be no more reason to fear this man," said Rick. "Then it's something to do with the murder. There are only two people I know of whom you'd be interested in to the point of trying to protect. Steve and your uncle. As you called Steve and asked him to help, it isn't Steve. Therefore it is your uncle. Therefore some enterprising person who knows damn well that your uncle is much too smart to pay hush money thought he could frighten some out of you. Am I right?"

She said miserably, "I'm not going to tell you."

"D'you know who this man is?"

"No."

"How are you to recognize him?"

"He said he knew me."

"What does he say he knows, Anne?" asked Rick. As she didn't reply, he went on patiently. "Your uncle strikes me as a man singularly competent to look after himself. Can't you see that this unknown is just playing you for a sucker?"

"Circumstantial evidence is sometimes more damning than the truth," she said, and added in a low voice, "particularly for Uncle."

"What have you been hearing? Has someone been telling you about something that happened before you were born?"

"You know about it?"

Rick sighed. "I told Mantle yesterday that he'd better

tell you himself, as you were bound to find out anyway, but he knew better, of course. What damn fool told you?"

"I've heard things, sometimes, before. A half sentence or something. Then last night, at the theater, Mrs. Rockwell was saying to someone, 'Everyone knew Mantle disapproved of the match, and as he got away with it twenty-five years ago, he probably thought he could again. Don't you remember the scandal?' She was behind the backdrop. I wanted to—— Oh, I don't know—I felt like charging round and asking her what scandal, what she meant. Then I just pretended I hadn't heard when she came round. Then this morning the man said, 'If he was accused of murder again, he mightn't be so lucky this time,' and when I asked him what he meant he said that everybody knew he'd killed his partner in 1922 and got away with it. I know Uncle didn't do it." She looked straight at him with sudden defiant confidence. "But I know what people are like. If there's been something like that in a man's past, they'll hound him."

"Not if he's worth fifty million pesos," said Rick cynically. "Suppose you tell me what this unpleasant bird on the telephone threatened to tell and to whom?" When she shook her head stubbornly, he went on, "What on earth d'you expect me to do if you won't tell me?"

"Just see the money paid so that he can't make more trouble in the future. And *please* don't ask any more questions."

"Sorry, Anne. Either you tell me or I'll take you straight to your uncle's office."

"No, Uncle mustn't know."

"One or the other."

"Domingo!" Anger flared up in her face. "Stop. The señor is getting out."

"The señor is not getting out, Domingo," Rick told him calmly. "Keep on going and go to the Señor Mantle's office. And don't argue about it."

"Domingo——" began Anne.

"Sh. That won't be dignified. This is a man's country, Anne, and they'll take a man's orders over a woman's." He took cigarettes from his pocket and offered them to her. She shook her head and turned away. Tears were struggling with anger. Rick lighted his smoke and said, "Either this bird knows that your uncle was missing from the room all the time during which the murder must have taken place——"

"You're making that up."

"I'm not, but the police know it too. Or else the bright lad has discovered that after you went home that night your uncle took the car and went out again, driving himself, contrary to his usual custom." A little gasp told him he was right. "And therefore your uncle has no alibi for the time during which Elting was shot, and the most tenable theory is that Elting was killed because he knew something about the murder of Deschamps. Am I right?"

"Do the police know all that?"

"Most of it."

She suddenly started to cry. He passed a handkerchief without comment and was aware that Domingo was frowning in mixed anger and perplexity. He said. "The señorita would like you to drive to Corrientes and Maipu and let us off there and park." Domingo looked round and Anne nodded her head using Rick's handkerchief for a forthright noseblow. "I hate making pretty girls cry," Rick went on, "but for your own sake, that had to be cleared up."

"I know Uncle didn't do it," she said after a while, "and I'm sure he'll be able to prove it. But he's had so many worries recently, labor troubles, troubles with the government; they've even threatened his life. And then he wasn't happy about Henri and me. And he isn't well. I've been worried about him, and I know Dr. Arrietti is. And he won't tell me what's wrong. They treat me like a child——" She broke off with a rueful smile. "I seem to have been behaving like one."

"There's no reason why you should know how to deal with blackmailers or other birds of that ilk," Vanner told her. "It's part of my business, not yours. You are going to do what I tell you?" She nodded and he went on. "I'll get out and walk down to the café and get a table. You come in and don't pay any attention to me. The man will either be there waiting for you, in which case he'll get up and ask you to come to his table, or he'll wait until you are seated and then come and join you. Either way, as soon as he joins you, I'll come over. Okay?" Domingo was turning the car up on Corrientes. When they reached the corner of Maipu and stopped, Rick looked at his watch. "Right on time. Give me long enough to get in and get a table, then come along."

Calle Lavalle is one block from Corrientes. Rick walked briskly along Calle Maipu until he reached the corner. The clean, unpretentious little café forms an L on the corner, the long line of the L down Calle Lavalle and the short one along Maipu. The entrance is diagonally across the corner, where newspapers and magazines are displayed on the doorstep by a man who doubtless pays a thousand pesos a month for the rights to that stand. It being too early for the evening papers, Rick bought a copy of *La Nación* and went in. He took a table by the window on the Lavalle side, from which he could see everyone who came in. There were several men alone at different tables. His eyes raked the place once with seeming carelessness and then he gave his attention to *La Nación*. A waiter came over and he ordered whisky. When the man brought it he paid immediately and returned to his perusal of the paper. But he was hardly more than three lines into the latest difficulties that the occupying authorities were experiencing in Berlin before Anne came in.

The various men who were alone all eyed her and quite obviously decided that she wasn't looking for a pickup; they equally obviously thought it was a pity. She stood indecisively for a minute, then went and sat down at a vacant table. A man entered. Rick had noticed him talking to another man outside as he himself had come in. The new arrival went straight across to the table Anne had selected, said something to her, sat down, beckoned the waiter, and ordered a beer. Rick swallowed his drink, set down the glass, and went over.

"*Con permiso*," he said formally, and seated himself in the chair between Anne and the man. "Now, suppose you talk to me about this."

The man shot an angry glance from Rick to Anne and said, "You were told to come alone."

"I said—talk to me," said Rick softly.

"You're interrupting a private conversation," said the

man. His nostrils distended like an angry horse when he breathed.

"The police don't much like blackmail and extortion," Rick went on quietly. "Let me see your *cédula*."

"I don't know what you're talking about." The man began to look worried. "I just came to get a packet from the young lady. That's all I know."

"Who sent you?"

"None of your business."

"Your pal who was outside?"

"None of your business."

"That's where you're mistaken," said Rick, and went on in English to Anne, "Ever seen him before?"

"Never!"

"Unless you want to answer a charge of attempted extortion, you'd better tell me what it's all about," said Rick.

"She ain't in no position to go to the police, not if she doesn't want her uncle in for murder."

"So you didn't know anything about it," remarked Rick. "You are a careless liar, and don't reach toward your belt. It makes me nervous whether it's a gun or a knife."

The man brought his hand up empty and laid it on the table as he stared into Rick's cold face. It was extraordinary how icy his gray eyes looked upon occasion. Evidently the man decided it was not a face to tangle with. He said, "I don't know what you're talking about."

Out of the tail of his eye Rick saw the other man who'd been on the sidewalk coming in. The two were very much alike. The second was merely bigger and older. He said to Anne, "Get up and go. I'll take care of this. Go to your car, drive home, and stay there."

"But——" she began.

"Don't argue."

She got up and turned, coming face to face with the second man. For a second she looked puzzled, then recognition dawned in her face.

"You said she'd be alone," said the first man.

"Not so fast, señorita. Sit down." The second man stood in Anne's path.

"The señorita is leaving." Rick's voice cut like a whiplash. So much so that the waiter, who had just set down the beer, stood and stared. "Go and get a policeman," Rick told him.

The waiter opened his mouth. He kept it open long enough to look at Vanner's cold eyes, then closed it again without a sound having issued from it. He laid his napkin carefully down on the counter and took a step toward the door.

"You'll stay right where you are." The bigger man's hand was on something that bulged in his pocket. The waiter stopped, teetering between a step forward and a step back, his eyes glued to the pocket.

Rick had stood up when he told Anne to go. Now he did three things in such rapid succession that they appeared almost simultaneous. The stein of beer was in front of the little man. With his left hand Rick knocked it into his lap. With his right he grabbed Anne and jerked her unceremoniously to his side. By that time his left hand was coming round in a semicircular swing which had a surprising power. At the last minute the bigger man saw it coming and tried to duck, but it caught him on the neck and sent him reeling off balance.

"Come on." Rick shoved Anne in front of him. The other customers were staring, but they showed no inclination to interfere. Rick pushed Anne through the door ahead of him. As he followed her a sudden blow almost numbed his right arm. He swore and instinctively grabbed his arm with his left hand.

"What——" began Anne, turning.

"Keep going," he told her curtly. In his left hand he held a small, viciously pointed knife. She hadn't seen it. He shoved it into his pocket. There was a jeweler's a few doors to the left on Maipu. Still keeping her ahead of him, he pushed her over to the doorway. "Go in."

She obeyed and went up to the counter. He followed more slowly and stood, leaning sideways against the counter, watching the street.

He knew rather than saw that an elderly man had come from behind and said, "The señorita wants to see some charm bracelets."

"D'you think they'll follow?" Anne asked in English.

"No, but I want to be sure. Who was the second man?"

"The chauffeur of the people who live two houses from us," Anne told him. "He's new, I think. They used to have an old man."

The shopman had placed some thin little chains with charms attached on the counter, and Anne fingered one after the other. The man brought some more.

"What will they do about Uncle?" she asked.

"Nothing." His lips curled thinly. "The last thing they want is to go near the police." He could feel a warm stickiness creeping down his right arm. He put his hand in his pocket.

185

"Are you sure?" She held up a bracelet. In spite of herself she smiled. "This little bear is sweet."

He took it from her, saw the little gold bear without ever really taking his eyes from the street, and said to the storekeeper, "How much?"

"Forty-eight pesos."

He laid a fifty-peso bill on the counter.

"But——" she protested.

"A souvenir."

"But I can buy it. I got money—before I came—from the bank."

"Go and put your money back in the bank and then go home and stay there. I'll see you to the car."

The man gave him change. "Shall I put it in a box or will the señorita wear it?"

"I'll wear it."

Before he went out into the street Rick stood for a minute in the doorway, like a man who is looking without much hope for a vacant taxi. Satisfied that all was clear, he said, "I think they are probably several kilometers in the other direction."

When he'd put her in the car, Rick looked round for a cab, and by a minor miracle found one, which he directed to Mantle's office. Being still lunch time, the place was practically empty. But Rick knew that Mantle usually had his lunch sent in. A small bald-headed man finally announced him.

Mantle was sitting frowning at some closely typewritten pages, the remains of his lunch on a tray beside him. His eyes narrowed a bit as Rick came in and he said, "What have you been doing?"

"Stopping your niece paying blackmail," Rick told him, and opened his coat. "Got any bandages or swabs round here?"

Mantle stood up, pressing the button on the interoffice communications system beside him. "Bring in the first-aid kit," he ordered. "Where's Anne?" he asked as he came round the desk and helped Rick off with the coat.

"I sent her home with Domingo and told her to stay there. She didn't know about this," he added. The sleeve, which was soaked, wouldn't roll up far enough.

"Better cut it," said Mantle. "I'll call Arrietti. His office is quite near."

"Hell, it's a new shirt," grumbled Rick.

The bald-headed man appeared holding a large tin box. He gulped when he saw blood and said, "*Qué barbaridad!*" He gulped again, dangerously, this time, put down the box, and bolted. "Call Dr. Arrietti and ask him to come," Mantle shouted after him. He turned out to be quite expert in first aid. He asked what had happened and Rick told him.

"The same *canalla* called me early this morning," said Mantle. "Asked how much it was worth to me to buy his silence. I hung up the phone. It never occurred to me they'd try on Anne. Damn their rotten souls." There was a curious intensity in the way he said it. "Why did you let them get away?"

Rick's face was inscrutable as he said carelessly, "Fuss—red tape—publicity."

"Only two ways to deal with blackmailers," snapped Mantle.

"Two?" Rick's starboard eyebrow went up.

"Liquidate them or ignore them."

"Liquidating is all right if you're sure no one else has the information," agreed Vanner. "Otherwise it's waste of time."

"Hanging's too good for 'em." Evidently Mr. Mantle felt strongly on the subject of blackmail. "Is Anne—very upset?"

"You've caused me a number of headaches today," Rick told him. "I said Anne would find out about the murder of your partner. It was the first thing these crooks told her."

"What did she say about it?" There was a definite effort to make the question sound casual, but all Mantle's experience and control couldn't disguise the anxiety.

"At the risk of repeating I told you so, she said exactly what I told you she would. 'Of course I know he didn't do it.'" Mantle was applying all his attention to swabbing with a surgical pad. "Leave a bit of my arm. I might want it. By the way, who did kill Downs?"

"The police never discovered who the murderer was," said Mantle.

"I asked you who killed him."

"It's the same thing."

Rick smiled. "To return to the matter in hand, where did you go when you went out by yourself that night after the Deschamps killing?" As Mantle didn't answer, he went on. "It must have been fairly urgent. You were in no shape to drive a car."

"I went to see the man I had watching Deschamps. I wanted it stopped and I wanted to be sure that the police wouldn't find out." He wrote something on a slip of paper and handed it to Rick. "That's his name and address. He'll confirm my statement if necessary."

"I'm sure he will."

The door opened and Dr. Arrietti came in. "What's the matter with Gonzales? He's being sick."

"Chicken-livered idiot," growled Mantle. "There's your patient."

In the way of doctors, Arrietti went to work without asking any more questions. Rick reached his coat to him and drew out the knife. "Old. Italian. That's what his accent was. I was trying to place it."

When the doctor had finished and been told more or less what had happened, Rick got into his coat and looked at the clock. "I'm late."

"It won't give you any trouble, but you'd do better to keep it in a sling."

Vanner shook his head. "Thanks for the first aid. Be seeing you at the *comisario's* powwow."

The doctor walked out with him. "Getting any nearer clearing this up?"

Rick didn't answer. Instead he said, "Before the dinner you were seen talking to Deschamps and afterward he seemed preoccupied. What was it about?"

Arrietti hesitated a moment. "You know Mantle has a heart condition?"

"Yes. I noticed it and he mentioned it. What is it?"

The doctor was learned and medical for half a block and ended, "He might live twenty years, if he's careful. Or he might go off like that." A snap of his fingers, dangerously close to the nose of a passer-by, finished the sentence.

"And . . ." prompted Rick.

"I think he was feeling ill even before dinner. He's been very anxious that Anne shouldn't know about it. He called me and told me to tell Deschamps, so that if he were taken ill, Deschamps would prevent Anne finding out. I said if he felt ill he'd better go home then. That I'd take him." The doctor smiled slightly. "He's a self-willed man. He just told me to do what he said. An argument was bad for him. So I did."

"He has stuff to take?"

"Carries it with him always."

"Why won't he tell Anne?"

"I think he's afraid she'd stay with him—out of pity. He couldn't stand that."

"No," said Rick slowly. "He couldn't stand pity."

CHAPTER 13

Dorothy Vidal had set the scene with care. She had on a long midnight-blue housecoat which set off her blond beauty. Her scarlet-tipped feet were thrust into blue-and-gold sandals. The curtains were drawn and a diffused rose light gave a warm intimacy. A log fire blazed in the hearth.

"It is *so* dreary outside today that it depresses me, so I had the curtains drawn," she greeted Rick. "Come in. You must be tired."

"I am," he admitted, and let himself be guided to a corner of the settee near the fire.

"How about a brandy?" She busied herself getting it, talking at the same time. "It really was ghastly alone here last night. The servants would be useless, of course, and anyway, their rooms are *miles* away and they'd sleep through an earthquake. Michel is so worried about me, poor lamb. You know, it all shook him up more than he admitted. He's been through such *ghastly* things, you know, and then to get in the middle of all this awful business here. It reminds him, you know." She handed him the brandy, settled herself in the middle of the settee, and then went on. "I understand it so well. There are things I can't bear to think about still. You people who were away on active fronts during the war, I don't think you can realize what it was like in places like this. You thought we had it easy. But the strain! It was worse, sometimes, for it was all cloaked under gaiety and friendliness."

The amateur theatricals certainly had lost something when Mrs. Rockwell had decided not to give Dorothy a part in the play, thought Rick. He said, "There was something I thought you could help me about. You knew Jean Fremont, didn't you?"

"Poor Jean," she sighed, and looked tragic.

"Poor?"

"He was a martyr."

"The French court thought he was a collaborationist," said Rick.

"Oh, the injustice of it! When every minute of the war years he was risking his life for his country! He loved it enough not to mind what people said! To stay with the Vichy regime so that he could help France!" She went on. It was a story worthy of any of the romantic writers of pre-1914. The gallant hero, risking his life and good name for his country, alone against armies, forsaken by his friends. She didn't miss anything. It was a pity some cinema script-writer wasn't there.

"He used to come here. He knew he could trust me. He came for sanctuary. For a few minutes' peace. Even my husband, who had called himself Jean's friend, turned against him. Jacques!" She gave a laugh which some dramatic school had probably labeled contempt. "I learned then what Jacques was! He turned against Jean, when among his own friends were men whom Jean knew were serving the Germans."

"It's surprising that Fremont's services weren't brought out in his favor by the court," said Rick when she stopped.

"Because the people who could have spoken for him had been butchered!"

"And in the investigation your husband was exonerated posthumously."

Her eyes flicked to him rapidly for a second. "Yes."

"The investigation by the French courts with respect to you is still pending." Rick picked his words carefully.

"It's just a matter of form, in connection with some funds I have there."

"Deschamps didn't treat it as a matter of form. He was having quite a lot of investigations made."

"Governments always do these things before they let a penny go. If you knew the *miles* of red tape I've gone through, just for a few pennies."

"And the result of the investigation will determine whether or not the government will release the money?"

"Michel says it doesn't matter and to let it slide. But why should I? I'm not afraid of the truth."

"You've known Fresne a long time?"

"Since he arrived here."

"You knew friends of his in France?"

"Someone gave him a letter to me. I've forgotten who. People are always arriving from somewhere with letters."

"What did Deschamps tell you about the investigation?"

"He was very polite and all that, but stuffy. You know,

193

like all government people. He had to have this form and those papers, and it would take I don't know how long."

"He was interested in your friendship with Fremont?"

"He mentioned that my name had occurred in the précis because I had French nationality on account of Jacques— my husband."

"He mentioned, too, that the records of the German Embassy listed certain sources of information under the name Vidal."

"My husband allowed himself to be used by men who called themselves his friends! How well Jean knew their two-faced dealings. But Jacques wouldn't believe a word against them!" It was quite dramatic.

"The extracts from the records that Deschamps was studying did not say whether the informer was Monsieur or Madame Vidal."

"Am I now to be persecuted too, for the little comfort I could give Jean?"

"Giving aid and comfort to the enemy," murmured Rick. "You too!"

He felt that if she had been familiar with *"Et tu, Brute!"* she would have brought it out. "But it would not be very convenient for you if the whole business were reopened and rehashed," he said. "First, it would interfere with your getting your funds from France. Second, it would not help your social life here."

"I should be vindicated!"

"Apparently Fresne does not think so."

"Ah, Michel! The money does not matter to him."

"No? Well, anyway, I take it you could use it. And

Deschamps was the one who was conducting this investigation."

"I forgave Deschamps. I understood. He had suffered too, but instead of teaching him understanding, it had made him bitter. He would not listen to reason. I could have convinced him that Jean Fremont was a patriot, that he lived day and night under the threat of death, to serve his country only to die in the end at the hands of his own countrymen. But Deschamps would not listen. He believed the lies!"

Rick got up. "Quite convenient for you that he died, all the same."

Dorothy Vidal stared at him. Abruptly she came out of her world of drama. She faced reality, suddenly. She faced the hard amusement in the gray-eyed man before her. She said slowly, "Are you accusing me of murdering him?"

"Accusing? No. I just said it was convenient he died."

"Why don't you find out what Howard Mantle was doing? He'd disappeared. He killed one man. Why shouldn't he kill another?" She stood up, spitting out the words viciously.

"Don't seem to like him."

"And Gloria Canning? Why were her gloves bloodied? She was Deschamps' mistress. Perhaps Canning had found out finally. Everyone else knew. Everyone's been laughing at him. Wondering when he was going to get on to it. Perhaps he had.

"Or perhaps she couldn't stand to see Deschamps marrying someone else. She'd never stop at anything to get her own way. She thinks with her dyed red hair that she can get away with anything. Even murder. She's sure she can do anything she wants with any man. And she's had plenty. Why don't you find out about her?" The words poured on in an ugly, half-coherent stream of hate.

"We are finding out about everybody," Rick assured her calmly. "Thanks so much for your help."

Perhaps it occurred to her that she was not letting him go with a very good impression, for she hurried after him and caught his arm. "You mustn't pay any attention to me. I'm nervous. Upset."

He detached his arm quite gently. "I won't," he said.

The desire for a drink to help him recover from the welter of melodrama, and a clean shirt, took him back to the Plaza. The porter told him, "There's a lady, Señora Canning, in the lounge. Señor Canning has also been several times. They did not come together." The porter had a dead pan. "Señor Canning is in the bar."

Rick said "Damn!" then he added, "Send me a straight whisky to the lounge and do not tell Señor Canning that I have come in."

Gloria was sitting pretending to read a magazine which she had open at a page advertising harvesting combines. As he happened to come up from behind her, Rick noticed it.

"Handy little things for the parlor," he said.

She started and turned a carefully made up but tired face to him. "I saw Douglas go downstairs. He didn't see me."

"He's in the bar."

"He—I—they——" She put her hand up to her head and said drearily, "I don't even make sense. Rick, they think he did it."

"Who?"

"The police. They seemed to know that I—that Henri

and I—they kept asking me if Douglas knew or suspected."

"And you told them . . . ?"

"I told them he didn't. That he'd been in the room, in the same chair, all the time when it must have happened."

"When you knew he hadn't been."

"Did you——"

"I knew."

"But he didn't—he can't have . . ." It trailed off in uncertainty.

"*He* thinks you killed him," said Rick casually.

"But how——"

"One of you must be wrong."

"What is it about my gloves? They kept asking me about my gloves, and Douglas lost them."

"Were they bloody?"

"Bloody? Good heavens, no!" She stopped. "Unless——"

"Unless what?"

"Somebody else used them," she whispered.

"Covering up in a murder case is shortsighted policy. If the party you're covering is guilty, it doesn't help. If they are innocent, it often gets them in a mess. I know it's useless as a rule to give advice, but I'll stick my neck out. Go and rest somewhere until it's time to come tonight and then tell the truth to both the police and your husband."

Rick watched her go to her car, which she had parked across the road, then he said to a boy, "Find Mr. Canning in the bar and tell him to come up to my room."

He'd found a clean shirt and taken off his coat by the time Canning knocked and came in. "Good God!" he exclaimed. "A *colectivo?*" The automatic instinct of anyone

197

who drives in Buenos Aires is to blame any kind of accident on the small busses or *colectivos*.

Rick laughed. "No. A knife. I don't seem to be popular." He was looking at his coat. "It was a new shirt and a relatively new suit." Without any change in tone he went on, "What did you do with Gloria's gloves?"

"Lost 'em somewhere. I thought I had them in my pocket."

"Have you been telephoning and calling all day because you wanted to come over and repeat the same fairy tale?" asked Vanner with a trace of irritability.

"I was very grateful to you for your intervention last night," said Canning stiffly, "though the police made it quite clear that they were not finished questioning us."

"The police like to be told the truth too." When Canning didn't reply, Rick went on. "It's a mistake to think that all police are fools. They know when you're lying. But they don't always know why. And when it's a murder case, they're apt to think that it's because you did it or that someone whom you're fond enough of to want to shield did it."

"The trouble with you is one never knows whose side you're on," said Canning wearily.

"I told you before, but you don't seem to believe me, that I intend to see this case solved. Meaning the person caught who actually stuck the knife into Deschamps and pumped the bullet into Elting. Not a scapegoat offered to the law. Nor any noble idiot sacrificing himself for someone else. Is that clear?"

A faint smile touched Canning's lips. "The truth and nothing but the truth."

"The whole truth." Rick had got into his clean shirt and was looking for the bottle.

"Bringing all the truth—if you mean all the facts—out into the open doesn't always achieve justice," Canning said slowly.

"Possibly not always, but a damn sight more often than a batch of lies and half-truths. Drink?"

Canning shook his head. He got up, his mouth momentarily tightening with pain. "What has happened has been my fault."

"You appear to have acted pretty much like a damn fool," agreed Rick. He'd poured himself a good healthy drink.

"The only decent thing would have been to give her her freedom," went on Canning.

"Did she ever ask for it?"

"No. But hell, I should never have married her in the first place. I knew it, really. But love is blind," he went on bitterly. "It makes one blind to one's own shortcomings, which leads to a worse mess than being blind to the other party's. I had no right to tie her down to a cripple. She thought she wouldn't mind. She was sorry for me. She wanted to do something to console the wounded soldier!" He gave a short laugh which hurt Rick to hear. "I should have known better. I did know. I was so much older than she. It was madness from the beginning. Madness and selfishness.

"I don't think I was really quite sane then. People used to come round to the hospital and give us talks about readjusting our lives. They meant well. Some of the fellows had the guts to face what their lives were going to be. I hadn't. And

I was luckier than a lot of them. There was one fellow——"

Canning was looking out of the window. After a while he went on again. "D'you know what it is to be afraid, Vanner? When you see something ahead of you and know you can't duck it and know you can't face it decently either. When your insides crawl and you haven't any pride left—any decency?

"I'd done a lot of boxing and been a pretty fair all-round athlete before. I suppose sports aren't really so important. They were, terribly, to me. I used to lie and think of that. No. I wasn't sane then.

"When Gloria came along, she was sorry for me. She mistook it for love. I told myself it was love. I hadn't even the guts to face that. I knew, but I refused to face the truth. I brought her out here, and I still tried to kid myself. I said, if she can go round and have a good time, she'll be happy. I knew the only decent thing to do was to say—we made a mistake—and give her her freedom. But I wouldn't face that either.

"Then Deschamps came along. I knew what would happen. He could dance. He didn't have to be helped out of cars, waited for going up steps. He didn't have to cancel dates at the last moment because he couldn't stand on his feet, or go home suddenly because he couldn't stand the pain. I knew. Long before Gloria. I've known what people were saying, too. I thought—well, never mind.

"One can't run away from things forever, no matter how much of a coward one is. They catch up with one. I should have done it months ago. A year ago. But it's not too late. She's young——" He was talking almost to himself.

Rick was silent for some time after he'd finished. At last he said, "Canning, do me a favor, will you?"

The man turned as if he'd almost forgotten him. "What?"

"Give me your word you won't do anything until after this powwow this evening?"

"Still playing God?"

"Will you give me your word?"

Canning took a cigarette from his pocket and lighted it. "I shan't be there," he said steadily.

"You'll be there if I have to keep you in sight every second until it begins," said Rick grimly.

"That mightn't be so easy." Canning's hand went to his pocket.

"Don't be a fool, man," Rick said roughly. "Nothing is ever gained by doing something without full knowledge of the facts. You think perhaps your wife killed Deschamps, and she thinks you did, and you're torturing yourselves and each other."

"She thinks—but——" Something that was almost the dawning of hope crossed Canning's haggard face.

"Do I get your promise?"

"Very well."

"Good. I have a couple of things to do." Rick finished his drink. Canning was standing by the door. "By the way, what in God's name did you do with the goddamned gloves?"

"I've told you." A wary look came back in Canning's eyes.

"Gloria wasn't wearing them during the time she was out of the living room while Deschamps was being killed," Rick told him impatiently. "I got that out of the maid."

"Then——"

"Then she didn't bloody them."

"I drove out along the Moron road, burned them, and scattered the ashes," said Canning. "I was afraid to use one of the fires in the house. I'd read somewhere that they can tell ashes and buttons."

"So that's what you were doing," murmured Rick. "Where was the blood on them?"

"Couldn't tell you. I'd just seen the blood and didn't look any further. I bundled them in my pocket and then I just soaked 'em in gasoline and burned them."

"It's people like you that make detectives overwork," Rick told him. "Coming down? Or want to stay here and finish the bottle?"

Jorge Seminario studied his gold watch chain as Vanner read through the reports on people's activities up until midday.

"There's no more about this man who called on Fresne last night?"

"No." Seminario reached over and looked at the report. "But Pablo is in the outer office. He is waiting to find out the results of the races. He spends all his money betting on the horses. He's never seen a race, as far as I know. But if he is off duty in the afternoon, he always waits here and telephones to see whether he eats tonight at Cabaña or Vascongada."

Pablo had one of the most valuable assets to a detective, complete ordinariness. There was absolutely nothing distinguishable about him. He looked like several hundred thousand men in Buenos Aires.

"Ah. The person who called on the subject. The person did not appear to be of a social position such as one would expect as a friend of the subject," said Pablo.

"Was he shabby?" asked Rick.

"He had a felt hat, very old, and not of good manufacture when it was new. A trench coat which was old and dirty. His trousers, that I could see, undoubtedly came from one of the cheap houses in the *Centro* where one may pay ten pesos down and obtain the suit on credit. His shoes, also, were of the cheapest grade, and moreover, the heels were worn down badly at each side. His socks were not such as would be worn by a man of taste. Furthermore, he badly required a shave. Altogether he was not a prepossessing person."

"Would you hazard a guess as to what he was?"

Pablo was silent for a while. "There are a number of men, señor, who appear to gain enough money on which to live modestly through the exercise of various dubious occupations. Some sell tips on the races." Instinctively Pablo's eye sought the clock, as if querying whether it were time to call to find out the result of some race. "These are usually valueless. Some are concerned with small operations in black-market currency. Others are engaged in peddling goods which have arrived in an irregular manner, such as cigarettes, small machine tools, perfumes, trench coats, silks, and so on."

"You think he might have been one of those?"

"He was of the general type."

"What about a hired murderer?"

"They are of the same type, señor. It is not a very profitable business. In view of the risks, I would say it is ill paid."

203

When Pablo had gone, Seminario said, "Mantle seems to have been interviewing the same type of gent. I put two men on his office, because it's hard to watch. My boy thinks he is using labor spies."

"He'd hardly have them come to his office, would he?" asked Rick.

"He says that anyone can come to interview him. He might trade on that and think no one would pay any especial attention to them."

"Fresne seems to have had some queer visitors at his *depósito* today as well," Rick said a few minutes later.

"My man thinks he's handling smuggled stuff. He said that yesterday from the *depósito* several hundred trench coats went out to be peddled. If they'd come in legally, they would not be peddled from store to store by canvassers."

A little later Rick put down the papers and said, "Call off your boys tonight, unless you hear from me not to."

"Think you'll have it solved by then?"

Vanner nodded as he got up. "It's solved now. The trick is to convince the police."

Seminario came to the door with him. "How in hell did the murderer get into Elting's building to kill him? None of the tenants let anyone in."

"Yes," said Rick. "Elting did."

He retrieved Sales's car and drove out to Olivos. He was wondering how he could persuade Anne to let him see the report on Deschamps which she had found. There were a number of things he wanted to know about that report. When he arrived, however, the problem did not present

itself. The manservant who came to the door looked doubt-
ful, and then Justine appeared from the living room.

"Anne came in completely exhausted," she said, "and
she's asleep. I did want her to sleep until the last minute
before we have to leave for the meeting."

Rick nodded. "How do you feel?"

"It's not giving me much trouble," Justine told him, and
added with a smile, "You're a good doctor."

"All the same, you didn't sleep," he said, looking at her
transparent pallor. He explained what he wanted and
waited for her to protest about looking at other people's
desks. Her dark eyes considered him but he couldn't read
them. No protest came.

"Have you been into the study? I'll show you. Mantle
has a suite of rooms downstairs. Had a bedroom and bath
built on a few years ago."

"Probably can't manage stairs," said Rick as he followed
her down the hall. She opened a door on the right and
motioned to him to go in. She remained standing by the
door, which she didn't quite close, her back to the room.

Vanner stood quite still for a moment, staring at the
painting that hung above the wide chimney. It was mag-
nificently lighted. A beautiful woman with a shadow in her
eyes. "I see what he meant about Anne's mother," murmured Rick.

"Beautiful, wasn't she?" agreed Justine.

"Anne's very like her."

She turned a little and nodded. When and if life ever
wrote its story on Anne's clear face, if something shadowed
her fearless eyes, Anne would be the same.

Vanner turned to the desk. On it stood a photograph of

the same woman, and beside it a miniature, obviously painted from the photograph. The room was more like a shrine to a memory than a study. Rick sat down at the desk. There were a few papers scattered on top. A seed catalogue, open at a page showing rose bushes. He glanced back at the picture. The woman had been painted holding a sheaf of roses.

The middle drawer was not locked. He opened it. A check made out to an *almacén* met his eye. This must be the drawer Anne had referred to. Another check was made out to the electric-light company. On the left were some typewritten sheets. He pulled them out. The name on the top of the stationery was the name that Mantle had given him. He started to read: "Confirming our telephoned report of 7 P.M. . . ."

Evidently Mantle had spared no expense on the job. Six operatives had covered Deschamps: two each, in eight-hour shifts. Halfway down one page he found: "Operatives changed owing to fear the subject had become suspicious."

He read it through, then replaced it carefully where he had found it. As he withdrew his hand he hesitated for a moment, then pulled the drawer out a bit farther. There was a .45 and two boxes of shells, one of .45s and another of 9 mm. A leather strap attracted his attention for a minute. Two circular straps with a strip between. The kind used for carrying a knife under the sleeve. Anne had said Mantle's life had been threatened. It seemed he was ready to protect himself. Rick closed the drawer and got up. Justine did not ask what he had found. She went into the hall. "This conference of the police chief's tonight. It will be so painful for Anne."

Rick looked at her sharply. Then he shrugged his shoulders a trifle and said, "Can't be helped, I'm afraid. By the way, I wanted to ask you. Think of Michel Fresne with a mustache. Does that mean anything to you?"

"Fresne?"

"He said something about St. Malo." He went toward the door. "Look out for Anne."

"I will," she said.

CHAPTER 14

Rick drove back to the Plaza at a rate considerably exceeding the speed limit and found a message from the *subjefe* and also one from Sales. He called the Police Central, but Señor Boggia was not there. "He tried to telephone you several times," a subordinate told him. "He was very perturbed about something."

"I'll bet he was," muttered Rick. "I shall see him at seven, anyway."

He called Sales's office and found he had already left. Telling the porter that he could be reached at the Farehams' telephone number, he went out and along to the Kavanaugh Building.

"You know more about police than we do," Louise greeted him. "What on earth are we supposed to give people? We've got drinks, of course. And I've made some doodabs." She pointed to two traps of cocktail canapés.

"Hello, Vanner." Fareham came out of his bedroom. "Louise has spent the day searching for an etiquette book with a chapter on how to behave at a murder investigation."

She made a face at him and said, "They didn't say how long it would take, and I can't have people starving in my house."

"You've got one right now!" Rick suddenly remembered that he had had no lunch. "May I?"

"Help yourself. Are you really hungry? If you are, I'll get you something more solid. There's loads of cheese. Roquefort. I don't think it's hopped out of the kitchen yet. It looked ready to. I was going to bring it in with crackers, but it stank so."

"If I might have the Roquefort," said Rick, with his mouth full of shrimps and mayonnaise. "Otherwise when your guests—or rather, the police guests—arrive, there won't be any canapés left."

"—and of course it was the maid's day off." Louise's voice floated back from the kitchen. "And not even murder or sudden death would make her give that up. Her boy friend was taking her to the *cine* to see *Murder in the Rain*."

"Much more interesting than murder in the apartment." Bob poured a whisky and water and gave it to Rick. "What on earth's going to happen, and for God's sake, why do they have to do it here? What are police stations for?"

"Don't ask me. I don't know how they do these things here." Rick took a drink. "By the way, the other night there were a lot of glasses ready with those sock things on, on top of the bar, weren't there?"

"I always have them put there, if I'm looking after the drinks," said Bob. "Once you've made a drink you fumble for hours trying to get the damn things on, and Louise gets furious with me if I don't do it."

"You're an awful liar." Louise appeared with a plate containing a hunk of Roquefort and bread. She had a knife in her other hand which was pointed perilously at her husband. "I just think it's a pity not to use them as we have them. And it isn't because of the furniture, because heaven knows, it's all marked up now. You've lived in France, haven't you, Rick? That's why I brought you bread instead of crackers for your cheese. It's so uncomfortable to hold a wet, miserably cold glass in your hand. It spoils the nice warming effect of the drink. Sit down and eat your cheese peacefully, and for heaven's sake tell us what we've got to be prepared for."

Rick, who had obediently sat and was already making inroads on the cheese, stopped eating and stared out of the window for a moment. "I rather enjoy looking for a murderer," he said irrelevantly. "But I don't enjoy the kill."

"Sounds as if you'd found him," said Bob.

Rick nodded and put some more bread and cheese into his mouth.

"Who?" they asked in unison.

"I'm waiting for the *subjefe*. He will have the last bit of proof I need."

"And you won't tell us?"

"I'd rather not."

"All I hope is that this powwow clears it up," said Louise. "I felt positively conspicuous in Harrod's today. People were looking. I could just feel them saying, 'It was in her house and she probably did it.' " She paused and said, "Anyway, I'll always feel guilty."

"Good God, why?" said her husband.

"Whoever it was, it's someone I invited, and if I hadn't invited them, it wouldn't have happened."

"I think if someone really meant to murder a man," said Bob, "they'd find an opportunity anyway. Don't you, Vanner?"

"Undoubtedly. Might postpone it but wouldn't prevent it."

At five to seven the *subjefe* and *comisario* arrived with several ordinary policemen who went into the kitchen. The *subjefe* looked undoubtedly perturbed, hardly managed to bow to the Farehams and thank them briefly for their co-operation, and then came over to Rick. He showed him a slip of paper with a name written on it and said, "I went personally and questioned the man. It is an all-night café. I don't understand. You do not seem surprised."

"I'm not."

People were arriving. First Dr. Arrietti. Then the Cannings, Justine, and Anne, all in the same elevator.

"Suppose you let me handle this for a while," suggested Rick.

Steve Sales came and said, "I've been trying to get you."

Señor Boggia bowed and said, "It will be an honor."

Mantle came in and went directly over to Anne. Michel Fresne followed, escorting Dorothy Vidal. Fresne looked round and said, "No police protection? Seems very slack to me."

"They do it better in Paris, I suppose," said Canning.

When they'd all settled down, Rick stood up and said, "As the *jefe* feels that you'd all rather listen to English than Spanish, he's asked me to explain one or two things to you.

"Owing to the number of people present the night that

211

Henri Deschamps was murdered, and to the amount of comings and goings between the bedrooms and the living room, the physical evidence was more confusing than usual, and it was more important in this case than in most to establish a motive.

"There were fourteen people at dinner. There were thirteen suspects. Because everyone is suspect in a murder case. Of the thirteen, some had no motive that so far has come to light. It seemed highly improbable that either the dead man's sister or his fiancée would kill him.

"No motives have appeared for Dr. Arrietti, Bob and Louise Fareham, or your humble servant. That leaves us with seven. Of these seven, one was killed in such a manner as to suggest a cover-up killing.

"So we had six. Douglas and Gloria Canning. Mme. Vidal. Mr. Mantle. Michel Fresne and Steve Sales. All these people had motives." Rick's eyes raked over his listeners. Michel Fresne was very white, his fingers playing nervously with his upper lip.

"You are all familiar with the irresponsible gossip which has been current concerning Gloria Canning and Henri Deschamps," resumed Rick. "I need not repeat it. It furnished a motive for either of them. Mme. Vidal had had some official dealings with Deschamps and he was not being co-operative about helping her to get her money out of France. Mr. Mantle opposed the marriage of his niece to Deschamps. Michel Fresne feared that Deschamps had recognized him. Steve Sales, as everyone knows, was in love with Anne. All these people had motives," repeated Rick.

"Some of them appeared to be somewhat inadequate motives for murder," he continued. "Until they were investigated a little more fully. Mme. Vidal had learned that Deschamps, before putting in her application for the transfer of her funds from France, was making an investigation into her wartime activity on behalf of Vichy and the collaborationists."

"It's a lie!" Dorothy Vidal rose dramatically. "I never helped the Germans! I've always been loyal to the Allies, to the true French, those who really served France!"

"Perhaps Mme. Vidal was hoodwinked by collaborationist agents," said Rick without much interest. "That is out of my province. However, even Mme. Vidal could not have been such a fool as to imagine that killing Deschamps would stop an investigation that the Embassy had started.

"M. Fresne had taken great pains to avoid the French colony here and the French Embassy. He came in 1945. Nobody knows anything about him before that. Except that he had a letter of introduction to Mme. Vidal, who, with or without her direct knowledge, had contacts among collaborationists. Also, he had Swiss francs sent to him here in 1945."

"I didn't kill him! I didn't kill him!" Suddenly Fresne's nerves broke. Sweating and gray-faced, he sprang from his chair.

"Deschamps spoke of St. Malo to him, and it was in St. Malo that Deschamps and his sister were arrested."

"*Mon Dieu!* With a mustache! *Comme je suis imbécile!*" exclaimed Justine. "The mayor! Jean Domerges!"

Fresne was staring at Justine with sheer panic written on his face. He wet his lips and tried to speak and backed away from her. Suddenly he found he could back no farther. The *comisario* was behind him.

213

"I've always known that Henri had seen the man who betrayed us, just for an instant, in the office of the Gestapo captain." Justine spoke slowly, her mouth twisted a little. "He was being paid."

"No—no. It wasn't I. It was someone like me, perhaps. It wasn't I." He looked up into her white face. It was quite merciless, the dark eyes hard and remote, as if they were seeing something that was past and could feel no emotion of the present.

"He said to me afterward, when I find that man, I will not give him to the authorities. I will do to him just what was done to me. And then I will kill him." Justine's voice was icy.

"Have pity!" Her cold white face with the dark burnt-out eyes seemed to snap something in Fresne's brain. "I couldn't help it. They got me one time. They threatened me. I couldn't help it. You must believe me. I didn't want to do it. Have pity! Have mercy! I didn't kill him." It was all rather revolting.

The *comisario* stepped forward.

"Arrest him for the attempt on Mme. Trinquard yesterday," said Rick.

"But——" began the *comisario*, then he saw Señor Boggia signing him to be silent.

"He did not kill Henri Deschamps or Fred Elting."

"I didn't kill him." Fresne's cracked voice went on. "I couldn't help it, in St. Malo. I didn't want to! *Mon Dieu,* you must believe me. I didn't want to! They made me." His voice trailed off as he met the stony eyes of the French-woman. He looked from her to Dorothy Vidal.

She got up, staring at him. "And to think that I——" she began.

"Be quiet," said Rick wearily, and went on. "Those were two motives that were stronger than at first seemed probable. Then there was Mr. Mantle, who disapproved of the marriage. But it went a little deeper than mere disapproval. Mantle had been in love with Anne's mother. Anne is very like her mother. Perhaps unconsciously, Mantle has transferred that love of her mother to Anne."

"Is all this necessary?" asked Mantle quietly.

"That is for you to say," replied Rick.

"You've got the murderer," said Mantle, and pointed to the shaking Fresne.

"No, Mr. Mantle, only a little coward who was afraid that if Mme. Trinquard recognized him or if her brother had said anything about him to her, that he might be accused."

"You mean he didn't——" began Steve.

"Kill Deschamps. No. He might have tried if someone else hadn't done it for him. Interesting speculation, that. Mr. Mantle. However. With several quite strong motives" —Rick resumed the manner of a lecturer—"the police tried once more to sift the physical evidence. On the floor in front of the dead man was an empty glass which appeared to have fallen from his hand. It had not broken, partly because it fell on a bath mat and partly because of its knitted sock or vest or whatever the things are called, which protected it.

"The investigation showed that the glass contained only soda. No alcohol. Mr. Mantle had said that he went to the study to lie down as he felt ill. Mme. Vidal saw him going

215

in. It was curious in such a small passage that he had not noticed Mme. Vidal. Mr. Mantle says he felt so ill that all he was thinking of was reaching a couch. Mme. Vidal said, 'Of course he didn't see me. He had his back to me.' If Mantle had been coming from the living room, he would have been facing Mme. Vidal, coming from Louise's bedroom. On the other hand, had he been going from Bob's bedroom to the study, he would have had his back to Mme. Vidal.

"Another question that puzzled us was Deschamps' absence from the room before his body was found. He wasn't in either of the bedrooms, in the living or dining room, or in the kitchen. No evidence has turned up to suggest he took the elevator down or upstairs.

"Unless he was in Bob's bathroom, in which case the late Mr. Elting, Fresne, and Canning were all lying, the only remaining place in the house was the study."

Louise, who was staring at Mantle, said, "But if he was in the study, how did his body get into Bob's room?"

"I think he was asked to go into the study. And that his murderer joined him there. I think he was asked to get a glass of water to take medicine in, from the bathroom tap, so as not to cause comment. I think then that he was followed into the bedroom and killed. Correct me if I'm wrong, Mr. Mantle."

"A fanciful story built on circumstantial evidence," Mantle said calmly. "You can't prove a word of it."

"Another interesting fact has come to light. The police have discovered that you telephoned three times between 4.30 and 5 A.M. from the Tripolitania café on Leandro Alem. It is about the nearest all-night café to Elting's Esmeralda apartment. Your desk drawer contains a box of 9-mm. shells."

"I used to possess a gun which used a 9-mm. shell," Mantle answered carelessly, "and I telephoned a detective from the Tripolitania. He will be glad to confirm my statement." He got to his feet. "Have we to listen to any more romantic fairy stories?"

An assistant of the *subjefe's* had been pouring a translation into his ear. Now he moved a little so that he stood athwart the doorway.

Mantle looked at Anne. And what he read in her eyes broke him. There was dawning understanding, loathing, and accusation. He stood perfectly still and for a long time he didn't speak. Across his face swept the knowledge that he had lost. Perhaps, also, the knowledge that he never could have won. For in the clear horror of Anne's eyes there was no compassion, no hope of forgiveness. She had got to her feet as if with some instinct to face this horror, which was beyond her comprehension, standing. Justine, who had been seated next to her on a settee, got up and put her arm round her. Anne didn't seem to notice. The older woman watched Mantle with eyes that were devoid of emotion. They held a certain cold, detached pity.

"It's horrible." Anne's whisper seemed to fill the room.

Mantle's eyes were very wide open. They seemed to be seeing beyond her. "Not a third time. This time I'll not lose you."

Perhaps the queer light in his eyes warned Justine. For at the instant that Mantle moved and whipped a gun from under his coat, she thrust Anne behind her and confronted him. "Madman! She's never been yours!"

For one second Mantle's crazed eyes rested on the contemptuously pitying face of the woman in front of him. Steve Sales made a flying tackle across the coffee table. Rick launched himself forward from where he had been standing by the bar, and the *subjefe* leaped from his position behind the door.

Sales's tackle had taken Mantle down. Rick got his gun hand. There was a report as the weapon went off harmlessly. With a strength unbelievable, considering his slight build, Mantle surged to his feet, momentarily breaking from Sales. He plunged toward the window. Rick caught him. Bob Fareham grabbed him from behind. Sales, on his feet again, got his other arm. For a moment, it was all they could do to hold him. Then, without warning, his body slumped. Sweat was standing on his face and his lips were blue.

"I've got him," said Sales.

"Get him onto the couch," said Rick. As Steve lay the now almost limp frame on the couch Vanner knelt for a second beside him, feeling for the heart. Arrietti came and pushed him away. He started to search Mantle's pockets.

"Don't want it." The blue lips framed the words.

Arrietti swore. "Hasn't got his medicine on him. Call the nearest—— I'll do it." He got to his feet. "What's the nearest *farmacia?*"

In a voice that wasn't too steady Louise supplied it. The doctor disappeared.

"Tell him, no use. I won't take it." The queer look had gone out of Mantle's eyes now. He just seemed unbearably tired.

Rick stood by the couch. "You'd received the detective's

report before you left home. You planned doing it. Why didn't you bring a weapon?"

"Why should I give you satisfaction?" asked Mantle with faint contempt. "You're only guessing. You could never prove anything." Somehow his eyes lighted on Anne, holding very tight to Justine. "It doesn't matter now." Pain shadowed his eyes and he looked back to Rick. "I did bring a knife."

"In the leather strap in your sleeve?"

"You found that too? Meant to do it here. Chance that Sales would be suspected. I was leaning on the shelf, getting some soda. Noticed the poncho pin. Seemed a good idea. But Elting saw me take it."

"How'd you get Deschamps to go into the study?"

"Told him I had to talk to him about Gloria——" A spasm of pain twisted his face. "How could he, when Anne—how could he?"

"And then?"

"You guessed well. Asked him to get water from the bathroom. Knew there was no one there. Could watch the door. I followed him. He didn't suspect."

Arrietti came back. "A man's bringing it right over."

Mantle shook his head. "I won't take it. . . . Elting thought he'd found a source of income for the rest of his life. He suggested we talk about it. The fool!" The breathing was becoming more and more painful.

Arrietti was looking in his bag and cursing. He filled a hypodermic. "We'll try this, but——" he said. "Where is that man from the *farmacia?*"

With a last recrudescence of strength, Mantle jerked his

219

arm away as the doctor tried to insert the needle in a vein. In a strangled voice he cried, "Elaine!" and was still.

The front doorbell was ringing frantically. Bob Fareham, who had been watching with a kind of fascinated horror, went. He came back with a small box in his hand. "Here's the stuff."

Arrietti closed the gray eyes and said shortly, "Too late."

The assistant had got behind in his translation, and the *comisario* and Señor Boggia were asking Rick questions. Two *agentes* were taking Fresne out. Rick answered the questions wearily. Someone had put a blanket over the dead man. They'd taken Anne into Louise's bedroom.

Dorothy Vidal, completely ignored, said, "I shall take measures to defend myself against these baseless accusations."

Louise, who had come out of her bedroom, said, "You left your coat in the hall, didn't you?"

Dorothy gave her a venomous look and tried to make a grand exit, but no one was attending. The Cannings were standing together, speaking to Fareham.

"If there's nothing useful we can do," Douglas was saying. "Want to go home. Gloria's mother's been upset about all this."

Canning walked with his careful, painful step to the *comisario* and spoke to him for a moment. Rick watched them go out. He followed and opened the door. They were standing in the little space in front of the elevator, waiting for it to return from taking down Mme. Vidal. Rick heard, "I've been such a fool——" and the rest of it was lost. The elevator signal showed that the car had come back, but they didn't notice it. They didn't notice him either. He stepped back into the apartment and closed the front door carefully. There was no need for him to say the things he had meant to say.

The telephone had been ringing in the study. Bob Fareham called out, "For you, Vanner."

He went in, picked up the phone, and heard, "New York calling Richard Vanner," and then a minute later a roar that nearly made him drop the instrument as Jefferson Sales's voice bellowed, "Why haven't you called me?"

"I've been busy," said Rick, holding it at a safe distance from his ear.

"As you're getting nowhere down there, I'm leaving for B.A. in the morning. I've chartered a plane."

"I hope you'll have a nice vacation."

"I'll clear my son if it's the last thing I do."

"That's all attended to."

"Why didn't you say so?"

"You didn't give me a chance." Rick put his hand over the transmitter and called, "Steve!" As Sales came in, he held out the phone and said, "Your father."

"I could hear him from the living room," he said as he took it.

Rick returned to the living room and started to eat the neglected canapés. Louise came and said, "Oh. Let's take them into the study or the kitchen."

Rick looked at the still form under the blanket and said, "If you like," with a slight smile and obediently picked up the plate.

Much later they were in the study. "Mantle was the only person at the party not drinking," Rick was saying, "though anyone might have decided that they wanted a glass of plain soda because they were thirsty or had hiccups.

"The only place where Deschamps *could* have been for at least five, if not ten, minutes before he was killed was the study. But Mantle claimed not to have seen him. Then Dorothy Vidal saying, without thinking, that his back was to her——"

"It still seems incredible," said Louise.

Arrietti shook his head. "It's a not uncommon pattern."

"One or two remarks he made at dinner showed that he felt himself competent to take the law into his own hands. He said, 'If you don't make your own justice, there won't be any.' And 'There's no question about it. We're in the right.' But, Steve, you supplied the key. You said he didn't much like you, and when I asked why, you said you didn't know but probably because you wanted to marry Anne."

"He's had enormous power," said Arrietti slowly, "and it has brought him none of the things he really wanted. I've known him for thirty years. Like so many people who wield great power, he could brook less and less opposition to his will as he grew older. He had got away with it in business. He grew to think he could with other things. I don't think he's been sane for years."

Louise shook her head. "I suppose medically it makes sense, but I still can hardly believe it."

"You knew, didn't you?" Rick looked at Justine.

"Since last night. They came back from the play. Anne was tired out. I was sitting by the fire. I hadn't been able to sleep and I'd been cold, so I'd come down. Anne came over to me. She was crying and I put my arm round her. It was so completely natural. I looked up over her head and found Mantle looking at me. I knew then. I was honestly afraid. I've never seen such hate on a man's face. He came over and pulled her away quite roughly and said, 'You'd better go to bed.' "

"D'you think La Vidal really was working for the Germans?" asked Bob.

Rick shrugged as he thought of the welter of melodramatic nonsense she'd talked. "I think she's got to a point of dramatizing herself where she believes her own stories. Any man who'd pull an 'I live dangerously' line could make her eat out of his hand. She may simply have been a dumb tool. By the way, there's one thing I want cleared up before I go, even if I have to ring the Cannings and ask. What was all the nonsense about Gloria's bloody gloves? How the devil did they get bloody?"

There was a moment of absolute silence, then Louise started to laugh helplessly. "No! I can't bear it! Were those gloves Gloria's?"

"Try and make sense," said her husband.

"The white gloves on the end table?"

"Yes. She'd left them there with her evening bag," said Rick.

"And someone thought it was blood!" More peals of mirth from Louise.

"Maybe we'll get it explained if we live long enough," said Bob.

"Ketchup!" spluttered Louise at last. "The shrimps with their little bowl of ketchup got spilled at the same time that the olives went over."

Steve and Rick took Justine back to her brother's apartment. Anne was staying with the Farehams'.

"Wonder what they'll give that louse Fresne?" mused Steve as they had a brandy.

"I think when the police start investigating his business there'll be some other charges against him," observed Rick.

"After the liberation he'd disappeared," said Justine. "We'd only ever seen him once, but Henri had an extraordinary memory for faces."

"The way he tugged at his upper lip suggested he'd worn a mustache at some time or other," said Rick.

"It's so ghastly for Anne." Steve had said it a dozen times before.

"She's young. She'll get over it," said Justine. Her eyes rested on Rick. "Just as well it worked out as it did. But perhaps you'd better flush the medicine down the drain."

Rick took a small box from his pocket and looked at it. He nodded. "Perhaps I had better."

THE PERENNIAL LIBRARY MYSTERY SERIES

E. C. Bentley
TRENT'S LAST CASE
TRENT'S OWN CASE

Gavin Black
A DRAGON FOR CHRISTMAS
THE EYES AROUND ME
YOU WANT TO DIE,
  JOHNNY?

Nicholas Blake
THE BEAST MUST DIE
THE CORPSE IN THE
  SNOWMAN
THE DREADFUL HOLLOW
END OF CHAPTER
HEAD OF A TRAVELER
MINUTE FOR MURDER
THE MORNING AFTER
  DEATH
A PENKNIFE IN MY HEART
A QUESTION OF PROOF
THE SAD VARIETY
THE SMILER WITH THE
  KNIFE
THOU SHELL OF DEATH
THE WHISPER IN THE
  GLOOM
THE WIDOW'S CRUISE
THE WORM OF DEATH

George Harmon Coxe
MURDER WITH PICTURES

Edmund Crispin
BURIED FOR PLEASURE

Kenneth Fearing
THE BIG CLOCK

Andrew Garve
THE ASHES FOR LODA
THE CUCKOO LINE AFFAIR
A HERO FOR LEANDA
MURDER THROUGH THE
  LOOKING GLASS
NO TEARS FOR HILDA
THE RIDDLE OF SAMSON

Michael Gilbert
BLOOD AND JUDGMENT
THE BODY OF A GIRL
THE DANGER WITHIN
DEATH HAS DEEP ROOTS
FEAR TO TREAD

C. W. Grafton
BEYOND A REASONABLE
  DOUBT

Edward Grierson
THE SECOND MAN

Cyril Hare
AN ENGLISH MURDER
TRAGEDY AT LAW
UNTIMELY DEATH
WHEN THE WIND BLOWS
WITH A BARE BODKIN

M. V. Heberden
ENGAGED TO MURDER

James Hilton
WAS IT MURDER?

Francis Iles
BEFORE THE FACT
MALICE AFORETHOUGHT